My Memories Dance

My Memories Dance

By
D.M.Hulme

ISBN-13: 978-0692029114 (D.M. Hulme)

ISBN-10: 0692029117

Edited by Garden Wellington Logan
Cover Design and Interior Design by Natasha Hulme

Published in 2014

I want to give thanks to Garden Wellington Logan and my mother Antoinette, for all of their help.

Extra special thanks, to my beautiful daughter Natasha, for her tireless efforts to make my dream a reality. Thank you for all of your help, right down to the book cover design. You are the light of my life and I could not have done it without you.

To my best and long time friend, June, who was the inspiration for the character, Ellen. Thank you for being my friend.

Life is not measured by the number of breaths we take but by the moments that take our breath away. - Unknown

Foreword

Sarah Walker, like so many other young girls in the Philadelphia Tri-state area, was so very lucky to be a child of the 50s and 60s.

The music scene was changing so quickly with the introduction of Elvis and The Beatles, Chubby Checker to Little Richard the new sounds coming through the radio changed a generation and dance shows like American Bandstand, Summertime at the Steel Pier and my very own show, The Discophonic Scene brought that music into living rooms across the country.

Philadelphia was the place to be for music and no other kid in the world could dance like a kid from Philly.

Being so close to the Atlantic Ocean meant many of us left the hot city and spent the summer *down the shore*. There are so many great memories and oh those Wildwood Days.

Amidst all the turmoil and strife that Sarah goes through in this book, she always tried to look to and remember the beat.

I love this story my friends and I hope you love it too.

Memories are precious fragments of time, which we keep safe in a lock box called our mind. Let them out often, for you are the only one who holds the key. Remember, you only rock once.

Jerry Blavat
The Geator with the Heater

PART ONE
Gotta Dance

My name is Sarah Walker and I am the only child of my parents Larry and Linda Walker. I grew up in Northeast Philadelphia in a close knit, working class neighborhood of row homes and tree lined streets.

For as long as I can remember I loved to dance. I would watch old 1930's and 1940's musicals, TV variety shows and wished to become a dancer one day.

Mom was a traditional homemaker of the 1950's and Dad worked at the Disston Saw Factory. He did not make much money and we pretty much lived paycheck-to-paycheck.

Dad also took care of his younger sister Betty and his mother. They both lived with us when I was first born. Dad got Betty a job with him at Disston's, where she met her husband and would later move out but Grandmom stayed. Dad was a loyal family man and a hard worker.

I do not remember my dad ever taking a day off from work. Even the day he came home for lunch, leaped over the white picket fence in our backyard and fell. The same fence he put up with his own hands the summer before. He only had a sprain, but he hopped back to work and never blinked an eye.

I grew up a pretty happy kid and my parents did the best they could. Mom would dress me up in frilly little dresses and put my hair in long curls. Every one would comment on how cute I was. When I would watch TV and see dancers, I would always mimic them, tucking the front of my dress inside my panties, leaving the back part of the dress hang down, that way it felt like I was wearing a costume. I remember doing this a lot.

In first grade, I discovered my ability to make people laugh. My first time on stage was at Hamilton Disston Elementary. I sat with four other kids on a bench dressed like a "garden flower." Being closest to the audience, I wore a ring of huge petals around my face, which was already funny looking. Suddenly, I felt the urge to pee. Wiggling back and forth, I could hear an occasional snicker from the audience. It went on for just a minute, but felt like an eternity.

My mother, now embarrassed, approached the stage, took my hand and carted me off to the restroom. As the door closed behind us I could hear the audience in hysterics. I was hooked. I knew I wanted to be on stage.

Christmas Day would be another opportunity for me to show my talents. My mother's relatives would all congregate at my grandparent's house where my Grandmom Sophie would cook the big Italian dinner.

It was 1956, the year Elvis Presley first came on the scene. I would lip sync to his records and did all of his signature moves. The family could not get enough and I would have them in tears from laughing. And I loved it!

Growing up it seemed we were the last ones to get everything. It took us a while to even get a telephone in our house. When I first got our phone, Dad said we were charged ten cents for three minutes and extra for anything over three minutes. So three minutes was the maximum I was allowed to talk each night.

My cousin Gail Parks lived in Bucks County, which is right next to Northeast Philadelphia, but to us it seemed like another country.

I was allowed to call my cousin once a year and in turn she was allowed to call me once a year too. It is hard to talk six months worth of conversation with your dad hovering and ready to tell you "three minutes are up!"

Gail and I were close growing up even though we only saw each other on Memorial Day, the 4th of July and Labor Day when my aunt would have family picnics.

We would write and mail letters to each other throughout the school year and after Grandmom passed away, Gail would come and stay two weeks at a time, once in July and once in August.

When Gail and I were six-years-old, my father's sister, Aunt Laura, and her husband Al, gave a birthday party for our cousin Edith. Edith lived right next door to us on Longshore Street.

At the time all of my cousins were girls except Matthew. Being the only boy, my aunt let him bring a friend. His name was Bobby Picknell and I fell in love right on the spot! I remember he had blond hair. I would never see him again except when I visited my aunt's house because there was a picture of Matthew's little league baseball team and in the front row was Bobby Picknell.

This started my blond obsession. I loved blond haired guys and later in my teens I would became a blonde myself.

As a kid I would love to wander off on my own and fantasize about my life and how it was going to be.

I would think about Bobby Picknell and wonder if he was thinking of me.

I would also fantasize about being a dancer. I dreamed of taking tap lessons, but Dad never had extra money and Mom wasn't the kind of parent who ran me all over wherever I wanted to go.

I never got the encouragement I needed from Mom. She always thought my hopes and dreams were silly. She is still like this but I have learned to shrug it off. In fact, I can't recall getting encouragement from anyone, not at home or in school.

Looking back, I could have been diagnosed with Attention Deficit Disorder (ADD). No matter how hard I tried to study, when I was ready to take a test, my mind would be blank. But, in spite of not doing well in school, I slid by and progressed to every grade.

A wonderful thing happened in 1956 when a new television show called American Bandstand started televising from my hometown.

Along with every other kid in the country, I ran home from school every day so as not to miss a minute of it. I would sit glued to the TV, watching the kids and picking up all the latest dances and dance steps. This came easy to me.

Soon, I had my favorite dancers, and watched their every move. I loved the couples especially Arlene Sullivan and Kenny Rossi, and Bob and Justine. My favorite teen dancers were Ron Joseph and of course, Jerry Blavat.

My good friend at school was a black girl named Ronda Claymont. Ronda was a great dancer. She and I danced every chance we got: before school, at recess, and after school. Every year there was a talent show and every year I was in it. My fourth grade show was an international theme. We had to learn a Spanish style dance number. We made our own costumes and even had a professional choreographer come in to teach us the dance.

He would come into gym class three times a week to teach the 12 kids he thought were the best dancers. The dance teacher asked us who the best dancer in the group was. My classmates all said me. This made Ronda angry because he agreed with the class and I became his partner to show the rest how steps were done. Unlike Mom, who didn't support my dream of becoming a dancer, he saw my potential, and I felt honored. Ronda got over it when she was put in charge of designing the costumes. We wore men's blood red button down shirts, black shoes and pants and we each made our own gaucho hats out of construction paper with little red pom poms hung off the brim.

The entire school show was great but we got the loudest applause. My smile was from ear to ear and there was my Mom and Dad clapping along in the audience as I stood next to Ronda, we all joined hands and took our bow.

When the new girl in our class named Amy Kelly moved only two blocks from where I lived, it meant that Amy and I could now walk home from school together.

You see, Ronda and Amy immediately despised each other and the possibility of Amy and I becoming close friends just wasn't sitting well with Ronda. Their dislike for each other made it especially difficult for me.

They each kept their distance from each other, more or less, but when they got into arguments they would both expect me to take the other's side. When this would happen, I would have nothing to do with either one, and then they both would be mad at me! I preferred this to having to choose and eventually Amy became the true friend.

Dancing became my life. It was the one thing I knew I was good at and there was nobody who was going to tell me any different.

With the popularity of Bandstand, my school had its first dance ever. I had never been to a dance and was overly excited and could hardly contain myself. That was until I got home and asked my parents if I could go. It was going to be held after school on a weekday.

The answer I got in so many words was - it would interfere with the time we ate dinner- and if that wasn't enough we also couldn't afford the admission fee.

Couldn't you just imagine my little heart sinking down to my feet? I just had to go or I would die. Don't they understand that? I was not going down without a fight. I had a few weeks to work on them and planned to give it all I had.

I waited a few days and tried again. I asked my mom but she still said no. This went on for a week or so and with time running out I had to pull out all the stops. I asked again the answer was still no and then I told her I would have to walk home from school all alone because everyone was going to the dance. Well that sunk like a balloon filled with lead. "I'll walk up and meet you at school and walk you home," was her quick comeback.

Then the day came. It was the day of the dance and I had gone home for lunch to give it one last try. "Please Mom, the dance is today. Can I go?"

Before she could say no again, I threw myself under the bus and offered this: "if you let me go I would only stay one hour then I will come right home. In time for dinner with you and Dad."

I must have worn her down because she gave the okay AND the money for a ticket. Happily back to school I went.

I approached my teacher's desk and told her I wanted a ticket for the dance. She said that they were all sold out.

"WHAT?" I said. "Is there any way I can get in?" She told me to go down to the gymnasium before the dance and see the teacher in charge of taking tickets.

After all of our classes, the dismissal bell rung and I went down with my friends to the gymnasium. Those with tickets all passed through the doors one by one. I went up to the teacher working the door and told him I had money for a ticket but was told the dance was sold out. The teacher told me to wait until all of the kids with tickets were inside.

I could see my friends on the other side of the door waiting for me. I was ready to burst. Didn't he know that the clock was ticking and my precious dance time was slipping away?

When the last student in line went inside he asked me for my ticket. I thought to myself, "Are you kidding me?" and I explained once more time that I don't have a ticket and that my mother just gave me the money at lunchtime.

"Sorry you must have a ticket", he said.

I began to cry. My friends were begging him to let me in. And I begged too, "Oh please can I go in?"

He must have felt sorry for me because he said, "Oh, go ahead!" and I ran past him only to stop quickly so that I could walk in making a stylish entrance. I doubt anyone noticed but the first person I saw, once inside, was a boy in my class that I liked. His name was Billy Leaver.

When I think of Billy now, all I can remember is that he was a strange looking kid. He had a flat round face, a pointed nose and small little teeth that slanted inward. He wore his sandy brown hair in a crew cut, but the top was longer, resembling a lawn that was in need of mowing, but I liked him just the same.

Whenever one of my classmates had a party we would always play "Post Office." It was a kissing game where each kid would get a number on a piece of paper. The boys would be odd numbers and the girls would be even. After a while of playing, you would know everyone's number and it became quite obvious who wanted kisses from who. I would always set my sights on Billy. I'd desperately try to guess his number and if I did we'd have to go in the closet together. It would always be a fast, small peck of a kiss before he dashed for the door but it was a kiss nonetheless.

Back at the dance I waited for the "ladies choice" song and I walked right over to ask him to dance. Paul Anka's, "You Are My Destiny" started playing from the speakers and as the music echoed off the glossy yellow bricks of the gymnasium, we started dancing.

Billy told me that it was his favorite song at the time and I was surprised, and whenever I would hear it, I would think of Billy.

I had the best time of my young life and never forgot my first dance and I stayed longer than the one hour I promised, and it was worth the consequences I had to pay.

I don't think Billy ever spoke one word to me the whole time we were in grade school, except when he told me that song was his favorite. Maybe he didn't like girls or maybe he was gay, although that would not be fair to assume. Boys at that age sometimes are just not interested in girls, right?

There was one exception... Frank Fox. Frank Fox was a real playboy at the ripe old age of 13 and I had a big crush on him during my last year of grade school. He had a crush on Joanne Richmond. My friend, Joanne Richmond, and he would talk to me to get to Joanne.

All the boys liked Joanne because she had huge breasts for a 14 year old. It was hard to compete with Joanne when you were a card carrying member of the "IBTC" better known as the Itty Bitty Titty Committee.

Frank Fox had coolness to him. His dreamy eyes, thick brown hair and full lips drove me batty. We hung around together a lot but remember it wasn't to be around me, it was to be around Joanne. If that's what it took to be around him, well so be it!

The day of graduation, I planned to ask Frank for a dance at the big party planned that night.

There had been rules laid out to us weeks ahead regarding our spring attire and what was acceptable.

Girls were not allowed to wear strapless dresses. Even spaghetti strap dresses were not allowed. So, when buying my dress, I stuck to the rules. My dress was gorgeous! It was turquoise with white lace over and a square neckline. At that moment it was the prettiest dress I ever owned.

At the party, I waited for Joanne to arrive with my friend Amy. I was also waiting for Frank.

When Frank entered the room he looked at me, smiled and said "hi," then walked to the other side of the room. Shortly thereafter, Joanne arrived.

As she approached us, we noticed she had changed her dress from the one she was wearing earlier at graduation. This new dress was white with little red polka dots. And it had, wait for it... wait for it... SPAGHETTI STRAPS that perfectly enhanced her big breasts.

One could not resist staring and I couldn't take my eyes off them myself. In an instant I whipped my head around to look over at Frank, who was already on his feet, making a beeline for Joanne. Every other boy in the room had their tongues hanging like dogs in heat but Frank was cool. Yes, his eyes were affixed to Joanne's boobs but he looked so cool affixing.

As he followed her all evening, I gave up thinking I had any chance with Frank and danced my little ass off, making the most of the dance. You win some, you lose some and I'm pretty sure nothing romantic ever became of Frank and Joanne.

☆

Grade school was behind me now. The summer before high school was here. Amy and I, along with her sisters, Jenny and Beth would go to the Bathy. It was an old Art Deco building that housed a huge public pool. It was about a twenty-minute walk from our homes.

The pool was enclosed in the building, but without a roof. There were lockers all around the sides, and out front there was a well-groomed grass lawn that sloped down where everyone could sunbathe. It was free to swim there, so that was where you'd find all of the kids spending their days.

Monday, Wednesday and Friday were designated for girls only. The boys had the pool all to themselves Tuesday, Thursday, and Saturday. Sunday was family day and nights were mixed boys and girls.

We would go every day, even on the boys' days. We couldn't go swimming but we could still hang out, sunbathe on the lawn and flirt with the boys.

Amy liked a guy named Raymond, whose nickname was Herky, short for Hercules because he was blond, tall and muscular with a deep cleft in his chin. Herky and his friend Johnny were bodybuilders and showed off when girls were around. They did handstands and other gymnastic moves and the girls loved it.

Of course I went because Amy had the *hots* for Herky, and I then started liking Johnny Palmer. He had reddish brown hair, and a split between his two front teeth. When my cousin Gail saw him she said that he looked like Alfred E. Newman from Mad Magazine, and he did a little.

After a few weeks Johnny started liking me too and one night he walked me home. Just before getting to my house, he kissed me. He was a great kisser, not that I was an expert on kissing at this time of my life but I remember it was damn good!

Johnny's family owned a jewelry store called The Ruby on Torresdale Avenue. It was the main shopping street for the neighborhood, with a Woolworth's, Tacony Shoe Repair, a bakery shop, dry cleaners, clothing stores, and hairdressers. Sometimes I would walk up to see him. He would come out and talk for a short time. Well Johnny and I lasted about three weeks and that was that. When you're a kid, you're fickle.

At first I wasn't allowed to go to swimming at night. I didn't know how to swim and my mother worried about me. I guess because the boys were rough in the water, but going to The Bathy, I learned how to swim, and even tried diving in deep end but I couldn't get the knack of diving. My beautiful and graceful start would always end in a belly flop for me.

The Bathy was getting ready for their annual water show, and this year they were doing South Pacific. Amy, her sisters and I tried out, and we were going to do the song and dance to "Honey Bun." We had to figure out all the moves ourselves. This is where I excelled, as I was good at dancing and choreographing the steps.

We were going to be sailors, wearing black rolled up pants, with our fathers' white shirts and sailor hats. We rehearsed every day. In the mornings, on the way to rehearsal, we would see an old couple sitting on their porch. At first they just smiled then it became a "good morning," then they asked us where we were going every day when we passed. We told them about the water show, and invited them to come. They were old and at the time they said that they would.

As we sang, one of the girls who swam at The Bathy played the role of Honey Bun. Her name was Irene and she was not only beautiful but could swim like a fish! I sometimes thought she was half mermaid. She did water ballet, while we sang and danced. The show was great, and the old couple whose name was Mr. and Mrs. Weeks, actually did show up and told us that we were the best. I introduced The Weeks to my parents and from that night on I was able to go to The Bathy at night.

Lincoln High School was exciting and terrifying because the school was so much bigger than my last school.

I always thought my three-story grade school was big but my new school dwarfed it and it took months before I could find my way around. I would have nightmares about forgetting what hall my locker was in.

There were lots of kids from Disston School at Lincoln, but none of them were in any of my new classes. Amy, Jenny, and I were still friends but we started making new friends too.

Amy and I did more things together than Jenny and I did. Amy was a year older than me. Jenny was two years younger.

I began to venture out a lot more, and to go many more places than before.

Some days I would ride the bus home with Amy, but on the days Amy had more classes than me I would go home alone. I enjoyed those days, where I would wait for the second bus. I would have to wait for it in front of a small run down luncheonette. The traffic at Cottman and Torresdale was always busy.

I would use that ride to daydream of how my life would be. I was a big dreamer! There was always a feeling, a comforting feeling that something good would happen to me.

I loved the ride home on the second bus. It would leave me off right across the street from my house.

On Saturday afternoons we would go roller skating. We went to church on Sunday mornings at Tacony Methodist and to youth fellowship for teens on Sunday night. It was fun. We would put on shows at old age homes and go to other churches in the area.

One year they had a big party at a huge lodge. I couldn't tell you where it was, but I do remember how excited I was when one of the older boys brought along a date that turned out to be my favorite dancer on Bandstand.

Her name was Joan Buck and I could not help but gush all over her. I told her she was the best dancer on the show and that I sent in a slew of postcards voting for her in the dance contest.

She thanked me because she, and her partner, won a car.

She was so sweet to me and we danced all night together. We did the Twist when Chubby Checker's song came on, the Cha-Cha, and we jitterbugged. She told me that I was a great dancer too, and coming from her, I was thrilled.

Amy was feeling a little left out and asked me to go with her to explore the lodge, so I did to keep the peace, but I would have been just as happy to spend the entire night with Joan.

It's another night I'll never forget. It's one of the stand out memories in my life.

It was around this time that I had my first boyfriend. His name was Evan and he was a bit of a bad boy. He would often get into trouble. It was not the typical boyfriend and girlfriend kind of thing. Seems when you're young, you tend to like someone new every other week. He and I liked each other some of the time, like when he would walk me home from school or we would meet at the movies. I would have to pay my own way then sneak open the side door to let him in.

I knew a girl from school who lived a few doors from Evan. She would tell me when he was sent away for doing something wrong.

From time to time he would be sent to the Youth Study Center where he would have to stay, then out of the blue he would show up again back at school.

This pattern went on until I was fourteen years old. Evan behaved like someone was flipping a light switch. Sometimes on, sometimes off. One day he would be interested in me and then weeks would go by without seeing him.

I would conclude that he was either locked up again or lost interest. He wouldn't call or write. He would just vanish and I wouldn't even think about him until he would appear again.

Amy heard that there were going to be dances on Friday nights at our high school's field house.

We went to the first one and it was great. Any place where I could dance was great to me. The only problem was, my parents would only let me go every other week.

In the early 1960's, another dance show started on TV. Summer Fun at the Beach would air every Saturday afternoon. I loved watching the kids dance but there was one male dancer who stood out from all the rest.

My eyes would comb the dance floor until I found him then I could not take my eyes off him for the remainder of the show.

After a few weeks of watching the show religiously, it would seem that I was not his only fan. He was getting bags of fan mail. The show's producers were cashing in on his popularity by spotlighting and talking to him. The host would read his fan mail on the air.

He was the most beautiful boy I had ever seen. Perfect in every way, and I became infatuated with him.

He was tall, tan, blond and he was a wonderful dancer and his smile just made me melt! I would sit mesmerized until the show was over and I sadly had to wait another whole week to see him again.

His name was Alex Bentley.

My aunt and uncle had asked us to go for a ride down the shore.

Mom did not want to go but Dad and I did.

I began thinking maybe I would see Alex Bentley there, dumb kid that I was. I thought they were dancing in there 24/7.

When we got to the Moonbeam Ballroom, where they televised the show, I ran over and tried to open the door but it was locked.

I remember the door had a huge split where the two doors came together so I pressed my face close and peeked in but there was no one there.

I was holding onto the handles of the door and suddenly realized that Alex might have touched that handle and I felt a strange connection I could not explain.

He became so popular on the show that in a year or two later he became co-host, and when the other co-host left the show, Alex became the only host. That made him even more visible to my eyes.

I went on with my secret obsession and my guilty pleasure.

I was a skinny kid growing up but from all the dancing, I developed some pretty nice legs, thin ankles, sturdy calves and strong thighs. I would get compliments on my legs all the time.

When I started high school, I'd always run into this one boy in the hall who would say, "Hey! There goes 'Legs Diamond'" whenever he saw me. Legs Diamond was a Philadelphia gangster in the 1920's but I guess that was his way of letting me know he thought I had nice legs. The next year he was in some of my classes and shortened his greeting to just "Legs!" As sexist as it would seem nowadays, back then I had a nickname and my best physical feature was the reason.

Concentrating, studying and focusing in high school was hard for me, so I started only attending only a few classes that I liked and would skip all the others. The classes I did attend I goofed off in and was the class clown. It always got me laughs but I also got in trouble a lot.

One such time was in cooking class. The classroom kitchen was at the back of the building and looked out where the boys would go to have a cigarette break.

On this day, the teacher left the room for a bit. I was looking out the window at the boys walking past when I saw my friend Tucker. I asked him for a drag off of his cigarette. He proceeded to put the cigarette through a small hole in the screen window and I took a drag when the door opened and my teacher returned. She asked me why I was at the window. I couldn't speak with a mouth full of smoke so she repeated the question.

Again not being able to hold my breath and the smoke in any longer, I let out a huge puff of smoke and all the girls in class began to laugh.

For the remainder of the class I had to sit and watch everyone eat and then I had to do all of the dishes alone, making me late for my next class.

Another time I got in trouble was in sewing class. I had a roster that included lunch late in the day and I was often hungry.

Before sewing class I would run into the cafeteria, which was nearby, to grab something to eat in class. There was no eating allowed in class but that would not stop me.

On a few occasions I did get caught. The teacher would take the food from me and lock it away in a closet. After class she would return it to me but I would put it in the trash. Lord only knows what was roaming around in that closet at night!

The teacher's desk was behind our desks and she would talk to us looking through a mirror that was the on the wall.

Once again, I would press my luck and stop to get a burger to munch on during sewing class.

I carefully tried to conceal it, taking a bite when her eyes went elsewhere. At that point I had only taken a bite or two and I saw her look up fast and right at me.

She got up from her chair and began walking in my direction. Thinking to myself that she was not getting her hands on my burger, I pushed the whole burger into my mouth leaving me looking a chipmunk harboring nuts for the winter. She looked down at me and said before returning back to her desk… "you're disgusting." Well this left the class in stitches. The teacher was not amused.

I had no luck in Math class either. On one occasion I remember my teacher bawling me out about something. I can't recall what I did but he was yelling and frantically waving a ruler. He hit himself in the mouth with it and his false teeth flew onto the floor. The class roared with laughter once again. This time I was sent to the Principal's office. It was not the first time I would visit the principal, nor would it be the last.

Like I said before, I had late lunch, so in order to meet my friend Mary, I had to cut class to go to first lunch. Mary had been a friend of mine from grade school. We became closer after we started high school. My cousin Richie would always see us together and asked if I would put in a good word for him. He wanted to ask her out, and wanted me to pave the way.

I told Mary that Richie liked her and wanted to take her on a date but she didn't seem too enthused. "Look just go out once, and see how it goes, and if you don't like him I'll tell him." She agreed to that.

Mary and I would dance in a room set up where you could go after lunch. There was a record player and Mary and I danced great together.

I would repeat the same routine at my scheduled lunch period with my friend Amy. It was a sweet set up until a teacher caught me in both lunch periods every day for months. I let greed blow my cover and the punishment was that I had to sit on the Principal's bench every morning for two hours every day before school started.

I wasn't the only student sitting on that bench. I remember many morning detentions sitting with this good looking Italian boy. He wasn't too tall and had nice features and dark hair, but was definitely not my type. Like me, he was failing all of his classes. Also like me, he excelled in just one subject. His gift was in Drama class.

He would get into real shouting matches with Mr. Kline, the boys' principal.

There were mornings where I would fear that fists could fly at any moment. I can still remember Mr. Kline walking back to his office after an argument. He turned and said, "Mr. Stallone, drop out of school and get a job because you will never amount to anything." Mr. Kline couldn't have been more wrong.

This was the same year I met Jimmy MacCarthy, but I called him "Jimmy Mac." He would be my first real boyfriend. His best friend was already dating a friend of mine, and told me that Jimmy liked me, so they kind of pushed us together.

I was 15 years old and Jimmy was almost a year younger than me, but we got along well and became inseparable. My parents asked what I saw in him because he was skinny with big ears and big feet but I loved him.

After my first year of high school, talk began of I-95, a new highway, being built. It would seem that our row of homes stood in the way and would need to be torn down joining hundreds of others along the State Road and Richmond Street corridors.

My East Tacony neighborhood could have been considered small being it was just an isolated pocket of two streets that had a row of two story houses anchored by bigger houses on the corner. Train tracks to the west and the river to the east also cut off my street, Longshore, and the street behind, Knorr, to the rest of the world. Bordering us to the north and south were Disston Saw Mill, factories, industrial plants and Tacony's only firehouse.

The train tracks would carry mostly cargo, but there was a passenger line up there too. Long before my time, it must have been an important hub to get to New York and downtown Philadelphia because there was an old hotel on the opposite corner that was fancy in its heyday.

It was kind of sad that all of the places where we played as children were no longer going to exist. Places like the lot behind my house where we played baseball and football, the old dilapidated hotel behind the lot where we sat on the steps night after night playing games like Truth or Dare, or large piles of dirt where we played King of the Hill would be all gone. Today, only a large pillar supporting the highway reminds me where my house once stood.

We moved not too far away, maybe a half of a mile but most of my childhood friends were scattered. The house that we moved into was much smaller, but nice, and in a nicer part of town. Amy, Jenny and Tucker all went to my high school but I would only see them before school, at lunch and after, as we had no classes together.

Thankfully, this move did not affect my relationship with Amy and Jenny outside of school. I still went to their house regularly, at least until a year later, when their family also moved into an apartment over Parisian Dress Shop on Frankford Avenue. I can still remember stopping there every morning before school, and having toast and coffee with Amy and her parents.

One spring night while I was doing my homework, the doorbell rang. Mom was in the kitchen doing dishes and Dad was resting on the couch after dinner.

I answered the door to find Evan standing on my porch. He had just gotten out of "juvie" and found out that we moved.

Evan was angry, I could tell. He asked me to come outside so we could talk. The questions started right away, asking me if I liked his friend Tony. I didn't skirt the issue. I was honest that I did think he was cute but I never went out with him. And so what? Evan never seemed that into me anyway.

"It's been over a year and you've hardly been around." and with that I started to walk back up to the porch.

That was when he came up behind me and pushed me in the dark corner of the landing. I could feel a slight pinching and realized he had an open penknife to my neck. I could feel the cold blade, as he pressed harder. I could see the fire in his eyes that I never saw before. He then whispered in my ear, "if I can't have you, no one will" Just then, my father came to the door and saw us in the corner.

Dad yelled, "what's going on out here?" and Evan turned and ran up the street.

I told my father that he was just trying to kiss me and I did not want him to. I said nothing about the pen knife until years later.

Three years would pass before I saw Evan again. One night before bed, I looked out my bedroom window. Across the way, behind our house was an apartment building and he was sitting in a lit kitchen window. We never ran into each other and within a matter of a few months he had moved out or got locked up and I never saw him again.

After I turned 16, I was called to the Principal's office. I hadn't done anything wrong this time so I could not imagine why. He told me to sit and he said to me "Sarah, you're not doing well in school and I'm sure you will agree with me on this." I looked blankly at him as he continued, "we think it's best that you leave and find work for yourself." He finished by saying he would try and see if he could set me up with a job and that he would get back to me in a week or so.

I left his office stunned. What about Jimmy? It will feel strange not being in school with him.

I told my parents at dinner what happened. Dad agreed with the Principal and thought it was a good idea too.

A few days later I was called again to the office and was told to report to a nearby department store for an interview. I went and waited but never was called.

Out of school, I felt isolated from my friends and my boyfriend, but Jimmy still loved me and nothing changed between us.

Every day I would look through the want ads and made a few calls but no luck. My dad saw an ad for Horn & Hardart, a popular east coast restaurant chain that was hiring so my cousin Rose, who had also left school, and I applied.

We were both hired on the spot but we were sent to different restaurants to work. I only had to take one bus to get to the restaurant. Rose had to take a bus and the elevated to the city.

I was hired to bus the tables. The job was okay but when I had all of the tables cleaned I would watch people eat. If I saw someone eating alone it would make me sad and tears would fill my eyes. Maybe they were all alone in life? Maybe they didn't have anyone. To this day, I still cannot watch anyone eat alone. It sounds crazy, but it's true.

After a few months the boss came to me and said that I was a good worker and he was pleased with me. He decided to put me in the servers line and with that promotion came a raise.

Two women working on the serving line were training me. Katherine, who was a short, middle aged woman with black hair, lived a few blocks from the restaurant, which was not a great neighborhood so she was tough and a little rough around the edges. If I took too long on my break downstairs, Katherine would get on the intercom with her scratchy tough voice and say, "alright Sarah, don't die down there." It was great for a laugh and soon we all would say that to each other.

Clara was my other coworker. She was a black woman with red hair who wore glasses and was a bit overweight. Where Katherine was brash, Clara was friendly.

Clara taught me how to flip eggs "over easy" in a frying pan along with flipping huge pans of home fries. Katherine on the other hand, showed me the weights and portions and how to change the pans in the steam tables without getting burned.

I loved it! Clara took a real liking to me and called me her baby, and I in return called her "Mom." She looked after me and made sure everyone treated me fairly.

Next to the kitchen was the sandwich and take-out station where Louise, a tall, thin black woman worked. She was in her 50's and was funny. At times she and Clara would bicker back and forth over the dumbest of subjects but in the end it was mostly to get us laughing.

My boss wanted me to learn all of the stations including desserts and coffee so I could fill in when one of the other women had a day off.

It was great for me because I never got bored. I would work from 6 AM until 3 PM. On the weekends when I would work, Jimmy would meet me afterward to ride the bus home together.

On my days off I would go and meet him after school.

Even though I enjoyed my job it still felt strange because most of my friends, including Jimmy, were still going to school.

I had signed up for church camp with the youth fellowship back before I started to go with Jimmy and there was no way to get my money back at this point so I went. I would be away from Jimmy for a whole week, and to a teenage girl who was in love, that's an eternity! Truth be told, the worst part of it all would be missing Jimmy.

We stayed in a dorm at Princeton University. While we were there, all of the Princeton students were on summer vacation.

We each had our own dorm room. The girls were in one building and the boys in another. My friend Amy's room was next door while her sister Jenny's room was on the second floor.

After we unpacked and got settled in, Amy and I went out and starting talking to some of the other kids who were there. They came from all over the country.

One girl in particular stood out. Her name was Carol and was attractive with the prettiest blonde hair I had ever seen. She wore black-rimmed glasses and I got the idea that she had "been around the block" a few more times than Amy and I had. Although it was a church camp, we were anything but angels.

That night at vespers, she leaned in and said, "If I don't get a smoke soon I think I am going to die! Do you smoke?"

At the time, Amy and I did smoke. Carol said she had some in her room on the third floor, but the chaperones watched us like hawks.

After everyone was asleep we would carefully and quietly make our way up to Carol's room. It was lights out by 11:00 PM so we figured by midnight it would be safe.

Everything was quiet while Amy and I climbed the stairs to the third floor, knocked softly on Carol's door, and soon we were sitting in a pitch black room with only three small orange dots glowing in the dark. We sat and smoked for what seemed like hours, until we heard voices coming from outside. We went to the window and across the courtyard were four boys calling to us from their dorm, "hey can we have a few smokes?"

We had no problem sharing but how would we get the cigarettes to them?

The boys vanished from the window and were gone for a while, but then they returned with a rope. After a few unsuccessful tosses from their window to ours, it finally reached. We put four cigarettes in a bag, clipped it to the rope and gave it a tug. They pulled the rope back and whispered, "thanks."

Just then, someone knocked on the door. Carol waited a few seconds then answered, "yes," in a groggy voice. The voice on the other side of the door asked, "is anyone smoking in there?" Carol answered, "no." The interrogation continued, "are you alone in there?" and Carol said, "yes, I was sleeping." The chaperone told her to go back to sleep and then left.

Amy and I were not sure going back to our rooms was a good idea so we stayed and fell asleep in our new friend's room.

The next morning Carol said she was going down to take a shower. Checking if the coast was clear she came back into the room and reported that everyone was going down to breakfast. While she was talking she took off her robe exposing her naked body to Amy and I.

I was a bit shocked. It wasn't because she was standing naked in front of me. I was shocked because I thought her pretty blonde hair was natural. Clearly her carpet didn't match her drapes.

By the end of the week, we heard rumors about her and the minister's son. She didn't let chaperones cramp her style.

At breakfast that morning, we made eye contact with the boys we gave the cigarettes to and we all had a good laugh.

Like everything when you're young and having a great time, the week flew by. It was a fun week and the day we left for home, we all cried.

We made so many new friends that we would never see again, but I was glad to be going home to see Jimmy!

Jimmy's prom was coming up. I didn't make too much money at my job so I couldn't afford a new dress.

My cousin Rose had just gotten married two months before so I asked if I could wear her dress. She said I could and as luck would have it her shoes also fit. The dress was white with shear layers of fabric on the bottom and sequins on the top. The shoes were white glitter heels.

I wore my dark brown hair in a flip with bangs and Jimmy gave me a pretty corsage of white and red flowers.

We went to the prom with a friend of Jimmy's named Ron and his girlfriend, Alice. We had a great time of course. It was the prom…nothing particular worth noting happened, it was just great sharing that event with him.

Life was going pretty good for me until one day I was called to the boss' office. He told me that he had to change my hours to a later shift, 11 AM to 9 PM.

I told him I didn't want my hours changed and that I was happy with the schedule I had. I begged him to keep things as they were but he said he had no choice.

All I kept thinking was "when will I see Jimmy?" My world revolved around him. He was my first boyfriend, so the thought of not seeing him everyday was devastating to me.

I told my boss I was sorry but I would have to quit. I knew my parents would approve because the neighborhood around the restaurant was bad and they would not want me coming home at that time of night. I missed the job and I missed my co-workers and mostly, I missed Clara.

From time to time I would go to see Clara and everyone else. They were always happy to see me. The chain started closing restaurants one at a time in an attempt to save the chain. Our restaurant was one of the first to close and I lost touch with everyone.

I still think about them today. I think about how everyone helped me and made my first job a great experience.

I was out of work for a while and I still saw Jimmy but something felt different between us. Jimmy was meeting new friends in school and even though he included me in everything, I was starting to feel alienated.

I was not comfortable around his new friends. I tried real hard to like them but there was always this feeling that they knew something I didn't.

Jimmy's friend Linda was having a picnic at her home. This day was one of the worse days of my life. Linda was a pretty girl and me not having too much confidence in myself, I was also jealous. Her wholesome looks, long strawberry blonde hair and sweet way she had about her, made me feel a bit drab.

She was sweet to me, and I saw nothing to make

me suspicious, but I was.

After that day, if Jimmy would call and say that he wasn't coming over my house I would fly off the handle and hang up on him but the next day all was forgiven.

This was happening more and more, until one night in particular I waited for him. When he did not show, I called his house. His mother answered the phone and said he was not home.

I asked her if she knew where he was. She hesitated then replied with an answer I knew gave her extreme pleasure. You see, she was never fond of me. She was always cold and always standoffish with me.

She made it seem that she cared about my feelings but I knew better. She proceeded to tell me that she did not think what Jimmy was doing was right and that I should know that he had been seeing Linda. He was going up to her house every night after leaving mine.

I remembered finding a transfer to a bus that passed her street and thinking, "why would he be riding that bus?" It was all clear to me now. How could he do this to me after three years with him? I thought he loved me!

A few days later was Christmas Day and he called to say he was coming over. I was thinking maybe he had a change of heart and it was me he really loved and wanted.

I was wrong. He came to break it off with me, and when he left I ran to my room and flung myself on the bed for one hell of a cry.

My mother came up to comfort me, telling me that he wasn't right for me. Comforting words, but when your heart is broken that's not what you want to hear, let alone believe.

I hated Christmas for years after that. It was only a painful reminder of a devastating time in my life, the loss of my first love. I had to face the next year without a job and a boyfriend.

I felt useless with nothing to do except lose myself in Harlequin romance novels. I preferred the stories mostly about the West. That appealed to me. I thought that was romantic.

Day after day I would sit and read, wishing a handsome cowboy would sweep me off my feet. How many more days could I waste?

When I was in school, there was one class that I was good at and that was Art. It was the only class that I could count on to get a passing grade in school. It was Art and dancing that I had the most confidence in.

I received a call from my old Art teacher. Before I left school, he submitted my work for a full Art school scholarship. He knew I was forced to drop out of school but called to tell me that I had been granted a partial scholarship.

I had to turn it down because my father just didn't have the money, not even half of the money needed for the tuition not to mention, the supplies. At the time I was still unemployed, so I couldn't pay anything either. My teacher was disappointed, but not as much as I was.

Later in life, when my father would see a painting or something else I did that showed my artistic talent, he would always tell me how sorry he was that I missed that opportunity. I would always just say, "oh Dad. Forget about it."

Once in a while, to get out of the house, I would visit my friend Amy, who was now married and expecting a baby. She had married a man much older than her, and I was a bridesmaid along with her sister Jenny.

Somehow I did not feel connected to Amy anymore. Our lives were so different now. I felt like I was suspended in space, with nothing to ground me or pull me back to earth.

Jenny called me one night after not talking for a few months. I would tell her all about my break up with Jimmy. And she felt bad for me just moping around my parent's house.

She started telling me about this dance that she went to and asked if I would like to go some Friday night. I thought about it. I remembered that after Jimmy and I broke up, Jimmy's friend Ronnie asked me on a date to the movies, but I was still distracted by the separation. The whole thing just felt too weird for me.

I told Ronnie I knew what he was trying to do, but I couldn't go out with him anymore and he understood. I thought maybe the dance thing might not work either. Even though I loved dancing, I missed and loved Jimmy more.

Jenny would not take "no" for an answer, "we're going Friday and if you don't want to stay…just say so and we will leave." And to that, I agreed.

☆

The dance was held at Concord Skating Rink about fifteen minutes from my house. The walk would take us past my old grade school, a huge brick building with a large chimney that could be seen from miles away, through streets of row homes and back driveways, up to "the Ave," past the funeral parlor in the big mansion and a few restaurants and bars.

This first dance at the rink, I would wear a white turtleneck sweater under a rust colored jumper with a drop waist and black belt with white tights and black Mary Jane shoes. My hair was shoulder length and I wore it the latest style, which was teased, flipped and rock solid with hairspray. I thought I looked a lot like Marlo Thomas in That Girl.

Back in the 60's there were dress codes. It was meant to enforce better behavior, but there were still fights now and then. Kids would be kids. I met Jenny at the roller rink, we got our tickets and went in.

There was a nice sized crowd and we danced every record. After a little while we took a break for a soda and Jenny asked if I liked it and if I was having a good time.

"Like it!" I said, "I LOVE IT! Thanks so much for dragging me out."

We went back on the dance floor, the next song they played was Jimmy Mack we both laughed and I sang "Jimmy, Jimmy, oh Jimmy Mack, don't really need you back!"

After that record there was a guest band playing live. The lead guitar player kept looking at me and smiling, he looked like Sonny Bono and although I wasn't attracted to him, I flirted anyway.

After the set, he came down off stage and asked me my name, and then he said he thought I was pretty. I had the best time that night I had forgotten that Jimmy had taken me away from all of this. This was me and what I truly loved. Somehow I had forgotten how wonderful it all was.

From that night on, my life opened up to many wonderful things. When a door shuts, another truly does open.

Jenny and I began going to the dances every Friday and Sunday night. My friendship with Jenny grew stronger. She was indeed a good friend.

She was in her last year of school and worked part-time at night during the week. Sometimes, I would spend the night at her house. This was nothing new as I knew her family as well as I knew my own. I spent many nights at their home when I was younger and friends with her sister Amy.

It's important to say that, although I loved Jimmy for the last three years, it never stopped me from watching Alex Bentley on Saturday afternoons. The show became my secret obsession and my guilty pleasure.

Even though I could only get my "Alex fix" during the summer months I became a loyal fan and sat, once again, eyes glued to the TV. He was everything I ever wanted in a guy.

He was my walking, talking fantasy and if I could have put it all in a blueprint for my perfect man, it would be Alex complete with a label that read,

"Custom Made For Sarah Walker!"

Alex was now a local celebrity and it was hard to find a person in Philadelphia, aged ten to thirty, who didn't know who he was. To me it was no different than having a huge crush on a movie star. He was so close and yet so far. One thing I'm sure of, whenever I would see him on TV, was that I felt a connection that I couldn't explain.

I was unemployed for a whole year when my aunt and cousin Gail had come to visit. Gail was now out of school and unable to find work too.

My father found a factory in the want ads that was hiring, and I was going the next day to apply. Dad suggested that maybe Gail could go too and if she got hired that she could move in with us.

My aunt agreed, and Gail stayed the night.

That night we washed our hair but Gail wanted a change. She put a dark brown rinse on her naturally blonde hair. What could go wrong?

It looked okay when we first got up but when she came from the shower it had turned the color of spinach. Yes, green hair! Panic set in and we didn't have time to do anything to change the color. We had job interviews to get to and we still had a 30 minute trolley ride to the factory.

As luck would have it, I had a dark brown wig from a Halloween costume. Wigs were in fashion at the time so it wasn't unusual to be seen in a wig. We were off to get those jobs.

As we hoped, we were both hired. Gail returned home for the weekend to pack and get her hair back to a normal color as we started our new jobs that Monday. It was going to be great working and doing everything together.

When we both reported to Levanthal's Casual Attire on Monday morning, the boss looked at Gail and said "didn't you have dark brown hair on Friday?" We laughed and just said it was a long story.

When we weren't assigned to the sewing machines, the job required standing in the same spot all day at a table, folding and packing women's clothing. It was hard on the legs and feet and in the summer months it was even worse.

Right behind the factory passed a train that transported cows to be slaughtered at the factory on the next corner. In the summer the smell was ungodly and the new girls would always get sick and pass out. Again I wasn't setting the world on fire with my paycheck, but I was working again and I was happy.

On Saturdays, Gail and I would go shopping for clothes and shoes for the dance. I just couldn't bear to be seen in the same outfit twice, so after we both paid my dad fifteen dollars for board, money for tokens to ride the bus to and home from work, and money to get into the dance, there was little left for clothes and shoes.

I have always been a slave to fashion, all my life, still am today and will always be. Within months, we both had a nice little wardrobe and stacks of shoe boxes. With any extra money, we would buy film for the camera and dress up in our latest outfits, posing like fashion models with hats, wigs, and jewelry.

One night, out of the blue I got a phone call. It was Jimmy saying that he was on leave from the Navy and wanted to see me. This took me by surprise, so I told him to call me the next day and I would let him know.

He was now engaged to Linda, but I thought this was a good way to get my revenge on her for stealing my boyfriend.

Isn't it funny how we never blame our boyfriends, we always blame the girl? If I saw him then he would be cheating on her. Score: even. I was pretty sure that I was over Jimmy by this point but I was still curious if any feelings lingered.

He picked me up in his car and we drove to the river where we parked. We talked a little about what he had experienced in the Navy.

Sitting there, I must admit, I was bored to death! How could he have been my whole world? Listening to him drone on, I felt nothing. Wait, that's not true. I felt a bit sick to my stomach. It was at this point he started to tell me how much he missed me and asked if I would I write to him.

I must have felt sorry for him or something because as he slid closer to kiss me, I kissed him back but I thought I was going to lose my dinner!

I loved him for three years and now not a thing! I told him I wasn't feeling well and asked him to take me home. Thank goodness we didn't have too far to drive. That night I knew it was time to start a new chapter in my life. Jimmy cheating on me and breaking it off was a blessing and what would come next would stand out to be the best time of my life.

☆

Gail, Jenny and I never missed a Friday or Sunday night dance. It was where I met my next boyfriend, Joe Clark.

Joe was a cute guy with blond wavy hair, hazel eyes and a real nice smile. I thought he looked a lot like Warren Beatty. He was about five foot six and had a solid build. We started dating, and Joe had a good friend named Lenny who we fixed up with Gail. They hit it off instantly and we doubled dated. Only problem was, Lenny did not go to the dances. Lenny was tall and thin, with brown hair and a nice face he was not only nice looking but a sweet guy too.

Lenny Jax only had one eye. He told us the story that at six years old he was helping his dad hammer nails when a nail flew up and stuck in his eye, he panicked and pulled it out and his eye came out with the nail.

Lenny adapted to his disability and was well adjusted. He even drove a car.

Although Gail was seeing Lenny she was juggling other guys on the side until one afternoon. Gail, after a day with Lenny, came home to find one of her other boyfriends waiting outside for her.

Trapped and stuck in the middle, it turned out the one guy did not like her dishonesty and didn't want to see her anymore but Lenny forgave her and she continued to see him.

In the meantime, the dances at the skating rink on

Friday nights were losing its crowds as kids were starting to go to a competing dance. We called it The Boulevard. It was a much further walk from my house.

The rink went back to skating on Friday but the Sunday night dances were still the place to be.

Sunday afternoons were the dances at Wagner's Ballroom.

It was hosted by Jerry Blavat, the biggest D.J. in Philadelphia, better known as The Geator with the Heater. We had heard a lot about him and his great dances and would listen to his radio show every Saturday afternoon. We decided to check out the dance.

I remember it was New Years Eve day 1967. Gail, Jenny, and I boarded the 56 trolley on Torresdale Ave. The weather was cold and overcast, and not long before we got there it began to snow pretty heavily.

The trolleys were known for not running well in the snow, and sometimes a heavy snow would cripple them indefinitely.

We stayed for a while and although we wanted to stay until the end, we were scared of getting stranded, and left about an hour later. But we did return many times after that.

Jerry Blavat would come down on the dance floor and dance along side the kids. He was a great guy. He is still going strong today, still doing record hops and spinning records at nightclubs. There are lots of familiar faces, a little older now, but his loyal following are still doing the Wagner's Walk.

Gail and I started frequenting The Boulevard on Friday night. Jenny would only go once in awhile as she was seeing some guy named Harold and it was getting serious.

The Boulevard was another old art deco building that housed a public pool, but was more like a country club. It had been there since the 1920's with its huge ballroom dance floor, complete with a mezzanine/balcony level. There were tall, thin doors that led out to small Juliet balconies with wrought iron railings that held only two people at a time. I never liked being out on those little balconies because they made me feel uneasy and dizzy.

The absolute best part of The Boulevard was the grand staircase that led up to the ballroom and the sounds of all the feet above dancing. It was exhilarating and made my heart quicken whenever I heard it. It was a sensation like nothing else, and I got to experience this every Friday night.

One autumn night we were walking home from the dance. The walk home was mostly down residential streets. Row homes and a few twin homes with front lawns. Some streets had big old trees and other streets had small or no trees. Many of these row homes were fairly new, only built 10 to 20 years earlier.

Jenny was with us this night when three boys were walking behind. They were saying mean things about Jenny, hurtful things, calling her fat and spewing obscenities. They were obviously drunk.

After a few minutes of this, Jenny stopped, turned around and walked up to the guy who was saying most of the insults. She told him to shut up and then said he should not drink because he doesn't know how.

In an instant, he gave her a shove. Jenny grabbed him by the front of his shirt, pushed him up against the wall and began banging his head several times. I could not believe what I was seeing. I had never seen this side of Jenny.

After this was all over, his two sidekicks walked away from him. He laid there covered in blood but was so drunk he probably didn't even feel what just happened.

I could only imagine what his head felt like the next day. I can remember Gail's eyes wide open, glancing at me in disbelief.

Gail looked at me when it was all over and whispered, "remind me to never get Jenny mad." You can almost bet that loud mouth drunk never opened his mouth to another girl again.

It was October of 1967 and Gail and I were still dating Joe and Lenny.

Lenny's cousin was planning a Halloween party, and just seeing the movie "Bonnie and Clyde," I was in love with anything that had to do with the 1920's and 1930's. That would be our costume. Gail and I dressed as roaring twenties gangsters.

We purchased toy machine guns at the five and dime store, and we wore pinstriped suits we found at a thrift store. And no 20's gangster was complete without a Fedora hat.

When we got to Lenny's cousin's house, I didn't know anyone. I was a bit shy when meeting new people, so I sat down on the couch alone. Gail, Lenny and Joe went into the kitchen. There were lots of people talking and drinking. I had never been a drinker. I didn't care for it much.

About fifteen minutes passed before Joe came from the kitchen and began making his way upstairs. I assumed he had to go to the bathroom. But then I saw a girl that had also been in the kitchen head upstairs behind him.

After my break up with Jimmy I wasn't the most trusting person, so you could imagine where my mind was going.

Gail came in the room shortly thereafter and sat next to me. "Where's Joe?" she asked and I told her he had gone upstairs and that I thought he might be with another girl. She said that they were talking to each other, but Gail thought Joe left the kitchen to be with me.

Gail had gone back into the kitchen to get Lenny. She sent him up to bring Joe downstairs. He immediately came back down. Lenny told me that Joe was not coming down because he was with that girl and they were getting high and making out.

Gail became angry and told Lenny to get him downstairs. "He came with my cousin!" I said, "NO! I don't want him to come down, just leave him where he is. I just want to go home. Will you take me home Lenny?"

The whole ride home I tried to act like it didn't matter that much but I was really hurt. Joe and I didn't make eye contact for months afterward.

Soon Gail and Lenny broke up too. Lenny "got jumped," beat up by a bunch of guys from his neighborhood. He was injured bad enough to be in the hospital. That's when it happened. When Gail went to see him, there was this other girl in Lenny's hospital room lying on the bed.

Lenny looked like a deer in headlights when she

43

walked in. The other girl made no attempt to get up and Gail simply said, "I'll be back later" but she never went back.

Gail and I dated other guys we met and things were going pretty good. We were still working at the factory together and going to the dances on the weekends. From time to time, Gail and I would go to her home for the weekend.

Her brother, my cousin Dave, was a real prankster! He idolized Mike Nesmith of the Monkees. He even wore a wool hat like Mike did and he did look like him. "A dead ringer," some would say.

It was a Saturday afternoon. Gail and I wanted to go to the mall to get outfits for the dance Sunday night. Dave agreed to drive us and pick us up later, for a fee of course. We each had to give him three dollars, and he told us to call him when we were ready to come home. We always had fun shopping and on this day we both found great outfits.

Gail called Dave and told him we were ready to be picked up and he said he would be there shortly. The temperature that day must have been at least 100 degrees and with extremely high humidity combined with the blazing sun. We sat in the heat for what seemed like forever and we did not even have money between us for a soda. Then Gail turned to me and said, "let's go, he is not coming. We better start walking." I asked if it was far and her reply was, "not too far."

It seemed we were walking for hours. We lived in what is called "The Delaware Valley." The humidity sinks there and sometimes you feel like you have to tread through it instead of walk. The heat and afternoon sun was not our friend. My clothes felt like they were stuck to my skin and I was getting weaker by the minute. Exhausted and dehydrated! I kept asking like a small child on a road trip... "how much longer?"

Although we were not close at all, Gail would just say, "not much longer."

Just at the point when I thought I could not go another step, things began looking familiar and I knew we were almost home.

Dave saw us coming down the road and jumped into his car. He drove up to us and he shouted from the window, "I was just leaving to come get you!"

Gail, pissed, sweaty and tired said, "oh sure you were. Thanks a lot!" I joined in and yelled, "by the way, you look more like Mike Nesmith's ass!"

Dave began laughing and drove off.

Once inside the house we dropped our bags and fell to the floor in the den. We were so tired and delirious from our ordeal in the heat. We thought we just needed a quick a nap. We fell asleep in a matter of seconds, right next to the stereo.

Dave returned about an hour later and saw us fast asleep on the floor.

As if leaving us stranded and heat stroked wasn't enough, he tiptoed in and put a record on the turntable deck, turned the volume knob up to full blast and went out to the yard. Looking through the window he switched on the stereo with remote control.

Blasting out of the speakers came Diana Ross' voice.

> *Hey life look at me, I can see the reality*
> *Cause when you shook me,*
> *took me out of my world*

I woke up, suddenly
I just woke up to the happening.

Both Gail and I couldn't imagine what in the world was going on. It sounded like a bomb went off. At first, all I could remember was being so disoriented and my heart beating out of my chest. Dave came in and acted all innocent. Gail screamed, "we know it was you!" He said, "what are you talking about I just came home."

When I think back now it was pretty funny and whenever I hear that song it all comes back to me and I smile. That night when we left to come back to the city Dave did drive us back home so I guess we forgave him.

One other prank Dave pulled was he had been to the junkyard and brought home a glass doorknob. He told my aunt that the man said it was from a haunted house. My aunt told him to get rid of it and that she did not want it in the house!

That night, he put the glass doorknob on her nightstand next to her bed and tied thin, plastic thread to it. He ran the thread down to his room along the floorboards.

When she went in to get ready for bed, he yanked the string making the doorknob fly across the room. Naturally my aunt screamed.

Of course Dave ran in to her room, "what's wrong?" My aunt said, "I thought I told you to get this thing out of here!" He told her he threw it out in the trash can in the yard and it must have found it's way back. She knew he was fooling her and after the fright subsided, she would laugh.

Dave would always do things like that. He still is a

bit of a prankster and funny.

After a year at work, we hit a slow period at the factory and Gail was laid off. That meant she had to move back home and look for work back where she lived. She did find work shortly thereafter but it was kind of lonely for me at first and I missed her so much.

I can recall one weekend with vivid clarity.

I was antsy and just wanted to get away from my house. If I didn't get away, I thought I would go mad!

I kept calling my cousin Gail on the phone but to no avail and as 6 o'clock at night came around, I pretty much gave up when suddenly there was a knock at my door. I opened it to find Gail. She and I had always had a connection. A real mental telepathy thing going on. If I would think of her or I needed her for something, she would pick up on it, and vice versa.

Gail and I also looked somewhat alike and people would always take us for sisters. We had similar facial features even though Gail had natural blond hair and hazel eyes. I was a bit thinner than she was and we were the same height.

She had gotten my "message" and had her boyfriend Bobby drive her to my house for a quick visit. I didn't even invite them in. I picked up the bag that I had already packed and said, "It's about time! I have been trying to get you all day, I'm spending the weekend!"

She said, "well okay, but we have to go back to Bobby's sister's wedding reception first. You can come if you want to." I shook my overnight bag in front of her face and shoved them out of the house and Gail said, "alright, lets go!"

On the ride to the reception she warned me. She said this was not a run of the mill wedding reception. First, it was being held in a funeral parlor of all places and when we pulled up, there were around ninety Harley Davidson motorcycles parked in the lot of the four-story building.

We walked in and Gail introduced me to the bride and groom who were decked out in the finest of black leather chaps and biker jackets.

We turned the corner and faced a large staircase where about fifteen guys were sitting on the steps. As we tried to walk by, one huge guy, about six feet six and four hundred pounds, picked me up by my waist and held me up over his head like a baby saying, "ain't she cute?" Gail, along with the other guys on the steps, was laughing her head off. He gently put me down and we continued up the stairs. I thought three things: this was the strangest situation I've ever been in, I'm the center of attention, and get me out of here.

Again we were stopped. This time we had to move aside to avoid another guy coming down the stairs on his butt. He had only one leg. His other leg was a wooden peg, just like a pirate in an old movie.

Suddenly we could hear a commotion coming from the third floor. Everyone rushing up to see what was happening passed us. When we got to the third floor there was a guy high on LSD trying to jump out the window. His friends were talking him down and after about ten minutes, they were successful but I was shaking with fear.

I looked at Gail and said "what the Hell? Can we get out of here?" She said we had to stay just a little while longer, so I went and sat with all of the older people in the viewing room until they were ready to leave. It was a scary scene but after we were safe we laughed about it often.

PART TWO
Dreams Really Do Come True

Business started to pick up again at Levanthal's. My boss asked if Gail was still available to work but she had already taken a new job closer to where she lived. I would have loved Gail to come back as the trolley ride in was so boring without her.

The next day a new group of girls showed up for work. I was asked to show a small group of girls around. Not quite training them, just being there in case anyone had questions.

I made friends with one of the new girls. Her name was Ellen and soon we both found out that we had love for the same things. In no time, we had a strong relationship. You would call us "BFFs" today.

Ellen had blonde hair when we met but within a few short weeks it changed back to chestnut brown. We were the same height and could wear each other's clothes. Two years younger than me, she was always happy and I loved being around her.

One of the things we did back then, and I'm not sure if friends still do it, was become blood sisters. It was done by pricking each other's thumbs with a needle until you draw blood and then pressing thumbs together which was symbolic of mixing our blood together, making us blood sisters.

At this point, summer of 1968 was looming on the horizon and the factory was soon to become a sweatshop.

There were large fans around the room but they

didn't do much good and the smell from the nearby slaughterhouse was nauseating, no matter how long you worked there.

We were all looking forward to summer and the weekends.

On Saturday nights we would go to the dance at Edgley Firehouse and Hall in Levittown, not far from my cousin Gail's house. On occasion, Ellen and I would have a hard time getting a ride to that dance. Levittown wasn't far from the city but getting there wasn't as easy as jumping on a bus.

I would take the 66 bus down to the Frankford Terminal to meet Ellen. Yes, I was heading away from the dance but that was the halfway point between my house and Ellen's. Plus, most of the time, someone with a car would swing by the Geno's down there and give a ride to anyone who was going to the dance.

On the nights they didn't drive by or we couldn't get to the pick up spot on time, Ellen and I would have to improvise.

We came up with what we affectionately called, *flagging geeks,* in which we would pick and choose from the passersby, who we wanted to drive us to the dance. A little like hitchhiking but we didn't jump in the first car to pull over.

We would wait for the guys who were nerdy and geeky to go past. You know the type...the bookworm, and the kind of guys girls just don't bother with. When they would stop for the light, we would flirt with them, lead them on a bit, and let them think they had a chance with us. All they had to do was drive us to the dance. They were always happy to accommodate.

We only had to flag geeks for the ride to the dance because once we got there we could always get a ride home, but one time we had two guys drive us, go inside the dance, wait for it to be over, and then drove us back home.

The strategy was in the picking of the right guys. The nerdier the better so we would be safe with them. Most of the time, they were just thrilled to be driving around with two girls that they were willing to do anything.

Of course, it wasn't nice on our part. Desperate times, well, you know the rest!

Once we got to the dance a friend asked Ellen and I if we were going to Wildwood on Memorial Day weekend. He added, "we're all going and the dance down there is pretty good too."

"Who's the deejay at that dance?" I asked and his answer was all I needed to make my mind up…"Alex Bentley," he answered.

I swear everything started to move in slow motion. I could not believe what I heard! I looked at Ellen and said that we had to go, she answered with a resounding "oh yeah we do!" As close as Ellen and I were, I had never confided in Ellen my feelings about Alex until that night.

I began daydreaming about how it would be when I finally saw Alex in person and just how perfect everything was going to be.

That Saturday before the trip I went to a new clothing store that just opened to see if I could find something to wear to the dance. After all, I was seeing Alex Bentley for the first time. I wanted to look good.

I began looking through the racks of clothing. I found a black and white romper. It had a high collar with round covered buttons going down the front, flared shorts that looked like a skirt and short enough to show off my legs but what I really liked about it was the back of the top. It was all opened except for a piece that went across just where my bra strap was, it was cute but just a little sexy. That was the look I always strived for. After leaving that store happy, I treated myself to a pair of white sandals too.

Memorial Day weekend finally arrived and the anticipation from weeks before that was eating me alive reached its peak.

We were finally on our way. When we reached the bus terminal there were hundreds of people our age boarding buses, all ready to let loose and have some fun.

This was my very first trip on my own with no parental supervision.

Sure there was the church camp years earlier but we were watched a little bit too closely. But on this weekend I was really free and on my own. I could do what ever I wanted.

Being the only child, my parents had a short leash on me but now I was twenty years old and working, they had to let me go on this trip. After all, I wasn't anything like a lot of other girls who got drunk, stayed out all night or took drugs. I was what some people would label goodie-two-shoes. I was so good it got on my own nerves, but my parents raised me right and I respected them.

Ellen and I were taking a huge chance going to the

shore on a holiday weekend without reservations, but Ellen was confident we would find a room. We were finally on our way. When we reached the bus terminal there were hundreds of people our age boarding buses, all ready to let loose and have some fun.

This was my very first trip on my own with no parental supervision.

Sure there was the church camp years earlier but we were watched a little bit too closely. But on this weekend I was really free and on my own. I could do whatever I wanted.

Being the only child, my parents had a short leash on me but now I was twenty years old and working, they had to let me go on this trip. After all, I wasn't anything like a lot of other girls who got drunk, stayed out all night or took drugs. I was what some people would label "goodie two shoes." I was so good it got on my own nerves, but my parents raised me right and I respected them.

Ellen and I were taking a huge chance going to the shore on a holiday weekend without reservations, but Ellen was confident we would find a room.

It was 9 o'clock at night. The sky was an indigo blue, soon to be black and filled with stars by the time we got off the bus. The smell of the ocean was liberating and we were thankful that we didn't smell slaughtered cow stench. We began walking, lugging our large suitcases in the heat of the night.

All of the hotel signs were lit up, "NO VACANCY" along the entire strip. It was not looking good for us.

Finally we could see a neon light that just said, "VACANCY." "Oh thank God!" I said, because I don't think I could have walked another block.

We walked in the door and an elderly lady led us up to our room on the second floor. It was just a small room, with two single beds and a chest of drawers with a small sink in the corner.

She started to recite the rules, like she has probably done for so many weekends in her life. She told us that there was one bathroom for each floor that everyone used.

She left the room through two old wooden doors that resembled tavern doors you would see in a Wild West movie.

I looked at Ellen and did my best Bette Davis impersonation, whirling around my cigarette, I proclaimed, "What…A Dump!"

Ellen laughed, "It sure is, but we were lucky to get this room."

We were sleepy from traveling all day and went right to bed.

Morning came. We woke up, got dressed and went to breakfast. I remember the day being so hot and humid that it was hard to breathe. "Oppressive" was a good word for it.

It was unusually hot for this time of year. It was more like August heat. By the time we finished eating breakfast you could hear a bad thunderstorm approaching.

We no sooner got back to the motel and the rain came down. We waited out the storm only to have another storm follow. This day was a washout.

We sat on our beds talking and reading fashion magazines that we picked up at the bus depot. As the storms battled it out all day it really didn't bother me. I always enjoyed storms.

I was, however, concerned that the storms may

continue into the night.

We had a long walk on the boardwalk to get to the dance and besides the dampness, humidity and rain, there was the sea air. A known enemy to my natural curly/frizzy hair!

In the late 60's, long straight hair was in which left me pretty much out! (I would have paid a king's ransom for the flatirons we have today.)

The wind-driven rain pelted the room from all sides we had to close all the windows. Did I mention it was oppressively warm?

The rain finally ended late in the afternoon, just in time to go out and have dinner and when we went out, we were caught off guard as the temperature had dropped about forty degrees, combined with the evening sea breeze and our light beach clothing it felt pretty close to freezing.

All of my fashion plans were quickly falling apart. My cute little open back outfit was now all covered up by Ellen's pale yellow jacket and brown moccasins now replaced my white sandals.

I put my hair in a ponytail and the only saving grace was a long black and white scarf that hung down to camouflage my curls that decided to rear their ugly little heads. I hated my curly hair and wished my hair was straight like Ellen's.

Not much was going as planned on this night but I was determined to have a great night no matter what I ended up looking like.

The walk to the ballroom was so cold I couldn't wait to get inside where I knew it would be warm. I turned to Ellen and asked if I looked okay. She answered, "You look fine".

Ellen and I walked into the building and across the

dance floor. My eyes couldn't wait to look on stage but I also wanted to savor this moment. It was something I dreamt about for years and now it was coming true.

Being in the same room as Alex Bentley and breathing the same air as him! My young foolish heart could not wait another minute.

Suddenly I looked up and there he was on stage, with bright overhead lights shining down on him. It almost made him look angelic. His bright white welcoming smile overwhelmed me. The way he stood tall in stature…if he were any more beautiful, my eyes would have burned completely out of my head.

I heard myself say, "he is gorgeous," in a trance-like state then I leaned over and said in Ellen's ear, "you can get that for me for Christmas." Ellen snickered like she always did.

As I walked closer to the stage, I was coaching myself to not look like a star struck little twit, which I'm sure he was used to. I told myself to just act normal and that he is just another disk jockey like at all the other dances I went to but that was so not true. There were times I couldn't resist and I had to sneak a peek at him.

Ellen and I were dancing front and center to the stage with our dance friends. Ellen started poking me telling me to turn around. Alex was calling me to come up on stage to dance with him. "Go on!" Ellen said. I didn't know if I could because at this point my legs felt like two overcooked strands of spaghetti and I was shaking like a leaf. I was star struck and wasn't sure if I had to pee or if it was just my nerves but there was no way I was letting anything steal this moment from me.

I reached the stage and began dancing with Alex. It was a Cha Cha and I couldn't tell you what song was playing because my heart was beating so loud I could hear it in my head.

When the song was over Alex asked where I learned to dance like that? I said that I just always knew how. He told me I was a real good dancer and coming from him, I was thrilled. He asked where I lived, if I came down the shore a lot, and of course, my name. Then he said, "you have got the cutest dimples!"

All I could say was, "thanks."

The song was over and he said, "Well thanks for the dance Sarah, I hope to see ya again."

I thought I would melt right on the spot. I don't even remember the walk back from the dance because I don't think my feet touched the ground.

The factory always closed down for a week in July giving us a mandatory holiday so on the bus ride back to Philadelphia we talked about going back for our vacation.

Later that week Ellen phoned a place called The Dixon Hotel and made our reservations for July.

I thought about Alex day and night and could not wait to see him again. In the meantime, we still went to all the dances on the weekends, worked all week, and saved our money for the shore.

The weeks flew by and finally we were leaving work to head to Wildwood.

Ellen's sister Sherry also worked at the factory and on Friday after work, she drove us to the bus depot.

On this trip we arrived at the shore around 7:30 PM. There was much more daylight left as Ellen and I checked into The Dixon.

It was a nice motel, much nicer than the last place we stayed. All of the rentals at the shore area were about the same though. A room with two beds, a chest of drawers, and a small sink in the corner, but at The Dixon, we had a large bathroom shower. It reminded me of a school bathroom. Again, much better than the previous place by far.

I called my parents to let them know that we arrived okay, Ellen did the same and we got settled in then, we took a stroll on the boardwalk, rode a few amusements, and had our portraits done in charcoal. We had to make sure that our money lasted all week. Money to eat and to get into the dance was priority one.

The next morning after breakfast, we went down to the beach to work on our suntans. We were both sun lovers and even at work back at the factory, we would sunbathe on our lunch break. We would smear our homemade tanning oil, a top-secret recipe only Ellen and I knew the exact measurements of each:

- *One bottle of baby oil*
- *Add iodine until the baby oil bottle looks like its filled with Red Rose Tea*
- *Shake*
- *After applying, spritz body with salt water from the ocean every 15 minutes or when you dry up.*

It never failed us. Throughout the day we would run down to the ocean and take a dip, and get relief from the heat. Then we would go right back to sunbathing. It was a vacation after all. The afternoons were devoted to the beach while the transistor radio played the summer classics like "Under The Boardwalk" and "Heat Wave" mixed in with the latest chart toppers.

The music that summer was made for dancing. In fact one hit song from the summer of '68 was "I Can't Stop Dancing" by Archie Bell and The Drells…

Music has a strange effect on me
It doesn't matter wherever I may be
Whenever I hear a drummer play that funky beat
I drop everything and get out of my seat

CHORUS:
I just can't stop dancin'
(Oh, no, I just can't stop)
I just can't stop dancin'
(No, no, no)

I would lay there with the hot sun, salty sea air, oil on my skin and sand between my toes thinking of Alex and how in only hours, I would see him again.

We left the beach in late afternoon for a shower and a catnap before dinner.

Alex was all I thought about for weeks. This was the one time I cannot recall what I wore that night. I guess there was so much more that I chose to remember.

The Dixon was only one block away from the ballroom so we were there in no time. We got our tickets and went inside. We met our dance friends front and center as we always did.

Alex was on stage sorting records to play, Ellen yelled up from the floor. "hi Alex!" He looked down and said, "hi Ellen, hi Sarah," and smiled.

Our friend Pauly had made up a line dance and we were the only ones who knew how to do it. Everyone was watching us and trying to do the dance steps themselves.

Alex looked down and was watching us. He jumped down off the stage and asked me what this dance was. "I never saw it before."

I told him that our friend Pauly made it up then Alex began to dance with us, trying to pick up the dance steps and he loved it.

After that, Alex took me back with him onto the stage. I was dancing with Alex! The song was, "I Guess I'll Always Love You" by the Supremes. Ironic yes, but I made sure to remember what the song was this time. When the song was over, Alex asked me if I wanted to go with him after the dance.

Now, what do you think my answer was?

Okay, I left you in suspense long enough…I said, "sure, okay." And then he kissed me.

When I came down off of the stage and returned back to the dance floor, Ellen said, "I saw that kiss!"

I could hardly believe it. Alex called me over again and said, "you might want to run back to get a few things."

I knew exactly what he meant and I would do just that.

"This is happening," was the only thing I could hear in my head. I couldn't remember my name, my address, my phone number, how old I was, anything. My mind was completely fixated on, "this is happening."

Somehow, I managed to get exactly what I needed for the rest of the night and the next morning. I packed my toothbrush, a comb, my bathing suit, underwear, a washcloth, and my makeup. "This is happening," was now set to music courtesy of the quick beating of my heart.

I gave myself one final glance in the mirror. The smile on my face was uncontrollably stretched from ear to ear, so I sucked it in, and ran back to the ballroom. This is happening.

By the time I ran back the dance was over. I told Ellen that I was going with Alex and that I'd see her later.

Was this really happening?

Alex packed up his equipment and we left through the back door with his two assistants. One of his helpers was our friend from the dance, Mike. He would always help Alex load his records into his car. I'm pretty sure it was Mike's desire to be a DJ too.

We went to a diner not far from the ballroom. I was floating on Cloud Nine and my nerves were off the charts. I couldn't tell you the name of the diner or even my middle name, but I was playing it real cool. I didn't want to eat so I just ordered a vanilla ice cream soda. He also had a vanilla ice cream soda along with a sandwich and chips.

We sat in a big booth and talked about ourselves.

Even though we were all sitting in the same booth, Alex and I mostly talked to each other, occasionally chiming in on the other conversations. We both made each other laugh and I started to feel comfortable. I was anxiously looking forward to being alone with Alex.

After we were finished we walked out of the diner hand in hand. I couldn't help thinking, at that moment, that every girl at the diner was envious and wishing they were leaving with Alex. It felt as though every girl was staring.

Mike left in his car with the other guy as Alex and I got into his white convertible sports car. It was a beautiful Pontiac GTO.

Alex rented a room for the whole season at a hotel at the southern tip of the island. I think it was called The Granada.

He led me up to the second floor, and into a small room. We stood in the middle of the floor, my arms around his waist and his around mine. He was so tall I had to look up.

"What sign are you?" he asked, as this was a common question in the late 60's. For some people, it was the make it or break it question and answer.

"Libra" I answered.

"That's October right? My birthday is in October too, what date is yours?" and I told him, "the 22nd."

"Mine is five days after yours." That made him a Scorpio. I didn't know much about horoscopes or the zodiac and I guess our signs were compatible to him so the subject was dropped.

He looked at me and smiled repeating from the last time I was down the shore, "I just love those dimples!" and with that we began to kiss. He stopped kissing me only to ask if I had to go back to my hotel.

I answered him willingly, "no I can stay with you, but would you mind if I took a shower?"

He told me where the bathroom was down the hall. When I went in and closed the door behind me, there was no lock. Slightly panicked I went back into Alex's room and said, "There is no lock on the door!"

He assured me no one would come in. Trusting his word I went back to the bathroom. Not feeling at all comfortable about the lock thing, I proceeded to get washed the best I could with one foot against the door.

I was very modest about my body and would have just died if someone had busted in on me while I was in the tub. I finished getting washed, touched up my makeup, brushed my teeth and returned to his room. I sat on the bed next him and he started kissing me again.

He got up from the bed and said, "I'll be right back, get ready for me."

I assumed "ready" meant ready to have sex, so I took off all my clothes and climbed into his bed strategically placing the top sheet just over my breast and private parts.

Thinking back now, I should have been proud to show off my body. At twenty I was lean, tight and hard bodied. You just don't realize it's never going to be better than it is at that age!

Alex entered the room and said, "well, aren't we the modest one?" and I quickly struck back and said, "Please don't make fun of me!" His reply to that was, "I'm not making fun of you, I think it's cute."

He took the sheet between his fingers and said, "Let's see what we have here." He peeled the sheet back slowly. The look on his face was putting me in mind of a young boy opening a package on Christmas morning.

Once I was fully exposed he went down, starting with kisses on my neck, moving slowly to my breasts and then lower down on my body. I could not believe all this was happening. Was I going to wake up from this heavenly dream?

It was not a dream. It was real and the sensation was like nothing I ever felt before. Fireworks on the 4th of July.

I began kissing his neck. I started to give him a "hickey" or "passion mark," as some people called it. A little trick we would use to mark our property. I really didn't want to leave a mark. I was only doing it to see if he would ask me to stop. Boys would usually stop you if they did not want other girls to see a hickey.

Alex didn't stop me, so I stopped myself. In my mind, he passed the test.

When it was all over reality set in. We made beautiful love together and it was better than I could have ever imagined. I slept in one of Alex's t-shirts. We kissed goodnight and turned out the lights.

The bed was right under the window and as I lay gathering all of my thoughts, I glanced over at Alex's naked body bathed in the pale blue glow of the moon. He was perfect.

☆

I had never seen a man fully naked before but this was not my first time having sex. Jimmy and I tried a few times, whenever I was able to steal a condom from my dad's drawer in his bedroom.

To me it was true what they say about guys with big feet. Jimmy had big feet and sex with him was painful. I'm not even sure we did it right.

I did have sex with Joe, maybe three times. Both Jimmy and Joe were never completely naked.

With Alex everything was wonderful. I wanted to stay alone in that room with him for the rest of my life. I drifted off to sleep next to the man of my dreams. This was truly the best night of my life.

In the morning, I woke before Alex and just laid quietly until he woke up. He asked me if I wanted to go and get breakfast but I declined saying that I should be getting back.

He drove me back to The Dixon and asked me for my phone number which I wrote on a small piece of paper he took from the glove box and in return he gave me his number. I thought, "this is promising," as guys never gave their phone numbers out to girls.

Maybe this all had some potential. We kissed then he said he would call me that week.

I told him that I was staying down the shore until next weekend. He smiled and said "I guess I will see you next weekend, then." I walked onto the hotel porch, turned, waved and watched Alex drive out of sight.

My head was still whirling from the night before, like coming down off of a drunken high.

Ellen was not in the room but I knew where she would be so I changed into my swimsuit and walked down to the beach.

I found her lying in our usual spot when she looked up at me, shielding her eyes from the sun and said, "Where the hell were you all night?"

I answered, "with Alex, you knew that!"

She continued in a disappointed tone, "I can't believe you spent the night with him!"

I got a little hurt by that tone of voice and the words coming out of her mouth. "Yes I did and what's the problem?"

She struck back, "Oh my God, jeez *Sar*, I don't know. I thought something happened to you when you didn't come back last night. I was afraid and I didn't know what to do. I was going to call your mom and dad to see if they heard from you, but decided to wait until morning and see if you showed up first."

"Oh no! I am glad you didn't do that! Look, I'm sorry," I said, but she just turned away from me. It made me feel cheap.

I said, "Come on. Don't be mad at me. I said I was sorry."

After a short time of silence we were talking again. The more I thought about the way Ellen was acting it became clear she was more jealous than mad. I laid on the beach the rest of the day basking in the glory of last night and was already looking forward to the coming weekend but make no mistake, I was going to enjoy this week with my best friend.

I was going to treat this relationship with Alex

with kid gloves. After all, he was a man not the young boys I've dated in the past and I was not kidding myself by thinking that I was the only girl Alex was seeing. This guy could pick up girls faster than a black wool coat could pick up lint.

Even though I was crazy for Alex, I'm sure for him I was just another conquest, a notch on the bedpost, an itch he had to scratch and the clichés went on in my mind.

Alex was a confident man and always gave off good vibes. One could tell he loved life and his job. He was always happy, smiling and cheerful. I never once heard him say a cross word to or about anybody. Who wouldn't want to always be near someone like that? But still, I built a fortress around myself and I was not going to let hurt get in. The week was going to be great, and seeing Alex Saturday night would just be the cherry on top of a weeklong delicious sundae.

Tuesday evening after dinner, Ellen and I were walking on the boardwalk and ran into Danny, a guy that worked at the factory with us. He said he was on his way to see a friend and asked if we wanted to come along.

Danny's friend's name was Josh and he was staying in a bungalow style house across the bay near a wooded area. He was a tad bit strange, a real hippy type.

Everyone was drinking beer from a can, even me. I was not a drinker, so I only sipped at mine all night. In fact, Ellen ended up finishing my can.

We sat around and talked as Bob Dylan records played. I'm guessing Josh was high on drugs because he was really "far out" so we left his place by 10:30 PM.

I suggested that we drive through the woods so we sat back and let Danny do the driving.

It was darker than any night I could remember. No moonlight and the huge old pine trees blocked whatever starlight there was.

Someone called out for Danny to turn out the headlights while we kept driving. He did and it was such a rush! He stopped the car and we just sat in the pitch dark.

Danny decided to take the experience to the next thrilling level.

When Danny turned off the ignition, you could see a million stars through the branches and leaves. He opened the glove compartment and pulled out a flashlight.

Holding it under his face he began to tell the story of the Pitcairn family. We already heard the tall tales of the prominent Philadelphia family and stories of their inbred watermelon headed babies with three legs, but then Danny started to freak us out.

When the news spread of a nursery full of deformed kids started going around, the Pitcairns needed a place to move the children to. They bought a huge estate in the New Jersey Pines where they hired a staff to raise the kids in secret.

The kids were developing as normal as three-legged watermelon heads could. They wrote letters to the Pitcairn family back home and the staff assured the mother and father slash brother and sister that the children were ready for them to visit.

They came out to the estate that night and

found the door wide open. When they got up to the second floor landing they saw blood stains on the wall that lead from one of the rooms.

When they went in the room they could hear a low moan coming from the closet. They opened the closet to find the nanny with her head hanging off. She was still blinking and moaning for help.

The Pitcairns ran to the car, but were surrounded by the kids. They attacked and began to eat the sister/mother alive.

The brother/father got in the car and sped back to Philly where he committed suicide by jumping from the roof of their mansion and it's said that the kids still roam the woods at night.

Just then, as if planned perfectly, something jumped on the hood of the car and all we could see were two eyes looking back at us. We were all startled, even Danny, who screamed for us to get the hell out of there. We didn't stick around long enough to find out what it was but our screams echoed through the woods for at least a minute before we all started laughing.

Thinking back it was a crazy thing to do. We could have crashed into a tree and because we were off the beaten path, we could have gone undiscovered for days. But we were young, living for the moment. Luckily, we all came through it unscathed and the drive back to the beach was a good time.

When we woke on Thursday morning it was damp and drizzling. It was not a day for the beach. We decided to walk around and look in some stores. I remember buying up a paperback book that was a controversial movie the year before. "I Am Curious Yellow" was sexual and considered revolutionary at the time.

Because I was curious, in any color, I bought the book and went back to The Dixon to read on the porch. Maybe because of its political nature or I just couldn't relate to the character of Lena because the political climate was that of Sweden's, the story really did not make much sense to me. I've never been interested in any politics. I did find myself distracted by the pictures of the characters in various sex acts.

I leaned my head back on the wicker rocker and let my mind drift to Alex. In only two days I would get to see him again.

Friday promised to be a warm sunny beach day, that turned into a pleasant evening but no sooner did the sun rise, it was setting over the bay. The day went fast, and thank goodness because Saturday was the day I was waiting for.

Saturday started early at the beach and lasted well into the afternoon. When Ellen and I finally left our dents in the sand and decided we had enough sun, we ran into some more friends from the dance. Pauly and Eddie waited until the last minute to come down and were now having no luck in finding a room.

The guys asked us if they could crash in our room, and we made it clear that they would have to wait until after the dance.

Ellen and I were taking pictures all week and we still had some left. We decided to bring the camera to the dance.

Everyone was there that night, even my ex, Joe. It seemed like every kid from Philly was at the dance that night, everyone but Pauly and Eddie. They never showed up.

I went up on stage to talk to Alex. He hugged me and gave me a kiss then asked if I was going to stay the night with him. I reluctantly told him that I couldn't stay.

I didn't bother to explain how Ellen got upset with me or that we agreed to allow two boys share our room with us that night. I promised him the next trip down I would stay with him for sure. He said he understood and I returned to the dance floor.

As we danced, out came the camera. We took some photos of Alex and all of our friends that we danced with. At one time during the night when Alex and I were talking, Ellen snapped our picture when he kissed me. It was a perfect moment captured on film.

I walked out to the deck, which was right outside the ballroom to get some air. As I stood there, leaning against the rail, I looked out where the black night sky met the black ocean water they seemed to melt together and all that was visible were the stars and white cap waves.

The sea breeze made me feel content and I began thinking how great the week had been and how it was almost over. We would be leaving tomorrow.

As my thoughts pleasantly drifted I had them rudely interrupted by a familiar voice. "So what? Are you seeing him now?"

It was my ex, Joe and to answer his question, I asked him, "what's it to you?"

"You know you could still be with me," he said.

That was when I figured out that Joe was the kind of guy that wanted you only when you were with someone else. This was a pointless conversation so I just turned and walked back into the ballroom and left him standing there.

Why in Hell would I want to be with him again? I was now seeing Alex and I wouldn't trade that for anything.

Yes, deep down I did have feelings for Joe. I don't really know why. He was a good boyfriend up to the night of that party but the truth was, Joe hurt me in a cruel way. It was embarrassing at the time it happened, it was disrespectful, and it was unforgivable.

Ellen danced over to me and said that a few of the guys offered us a ride back to Philly tomorrow. I thought that it was a relief as it beat taking the bus.

After the dance, we returned to The Dixon. Pauly or Eddie still were nowhere to be found. We waited on the porch for a while to see if they would show up.

It wasn't too long after we sat down and they both came staggering up the street and talking loudly. It was obvious they were drinking or high.

"SHHH! Keep it down, will ya? You'll get us kicked out and all four of us will have no place to sleep!"

Ellen went in first to see if anyone was at the desk. She signaled to me that all was clear and the three of us went up the side staircase until we reached our floor then ran to our room.

We pulled the mattresses off the bed on to the floor where Ellen and I slept and the guys slept on the box springs. They were bombed and we were tired from the dance so everyone pretty much went right to sleep.

We woke them up early so they could get out without being seen. "Thanks! You girls are the best!" they said before being on their way.

After breakfast, Ellen and I started to pack up our things and then sat on the porch until 1 o'clock when we left to meet our ride.

They were parked and waiting for us. We put our luggage in the trunk of the car. Ellen sat in the front and I got in the back. We were waiting for one more person and if he was not there by 1:30, we were leaving.

The back door suddenly swung open and a body flung itself in and across the bodies of me and the other guy sitting in the back seat. It was like he was rolling on a conveyer belt until his head hit my lap.

It was my ex, Joe and he was completely hung over but now had comfortably "made his bed" for the ride home!

All I could think to myself was, "we should have taken the bus home."

The car had no air-conditioning and every time we stopped, the heat was unbearable. And as if that wasn't bad enough, I had someone lying on me for the two hour ride home.

I asked if anyone was going to the dance at the rink that night and the answer was a disappointing but resounding "No!" followed by, "are you nuts?" "in this heat?" and "we're broke!"

I was dropped off two blocks from my house, which was okay. They didn't need to go out of their way.

It was almost 4 o'clock in the afternoon on a Sunday in mid-July and I could remember how eerily quiet it was. As if I was the only person left on Earth. It was so hot, there was not another soul on the street. You could actually see the heat and haze in the air.

I was so happy to see my parents. I couldn't believe how much I missed them regardless of all of the fun I was having at the shore.

After dinner, I went to my room to unpack. Putting my things away, the reality of returning to work set in and after a week like that, it would be a little tough getting back in the groove again.

I knew there would be many more weekends down the shore and for that I would need money and that means keeping my job.

In the weeks to come, I thought a lot about those 10 days in Wildwood and I finally felt good about myself. I felt confident and powerful and I felt like somebody.

It was because of Alex that I felt this way. If I was worthy of his attention, I couldn't be all that bad, right?

Alex and I talked on the phone a few times in the following weeks, and I always felt good when he called.

I never called him though, I just never felt comfortable doing so.

Ellen and I arranged to go back to the shore the third weekend in August. I planned to keep my In the weeks to come, I thought a lot about those 10 days in Wildwood and I finally felt good about myself. I felt confident and powerful and I felt like somebody.

It was because of Alex that I felt this way. If I was worthy of his attention, I couldn't be all that bad, right?

Alex and I talked on the phone a few times in the following weeks, and I always felt good when he called. I never called him though, I just never felt comfortable doing so.

Ellen and I arranged to go back to the shore the third weekend in August. I planned to keep my promise to stay with Alex but I neglected to tell him when we talked on the phone.

I wanted to see what would happen if I showed up and caught him by surprise. It was another trap. I needed to know Alex's true feelings for me. I would not let myself get hurt again.

Ellen broke the bad news Thursday morning at work that she couldn't go down the shore. She had to watch her sister's kids and it was last minute.

I felt as if someone pulled the rug out from under me. I began to think of who I could get to go with me?

That night after dinner, I called Jenny to see if she was available. She was getting married in a few weeks and was far too busy. I called Gail, but she couldn't get off from work on such short notice.

I wasn't used to going places alone. I couldn't see the fun in it. But I wouldn't really be alone. I'd be with Alex.

Friday afternoon at work I was talking to Danny and asked if by any chance he was going to the shore for the weekend. To my surprise he said that he was. I asked if he would mind if I joined him for the ride down and back. He said that he would enjoy the company and picked me up at my house at 7 PM. I had to lie to my parents by saying we were picking up Ellen next.

Danny dropped me off at the hotel. I had reservations but it was much further from the beach than The Dixon. I tried to reserve at The Dixon but was unable to get a room on this weekend.

It was about 9:30 PM when I checked in.

I didn't go out. I just laid on the bed, missing my friend Ellen. It felt funny being there without her. Instead, I was alone and the only thing keeping me from crying was thinking of being with Alex the next night.

It was hard but I finally fell asleep and the next morning I went to breakfast alone. I felt much like one of those pitiful people that would bring me to tears at the restaurant where I worked so many years before.

I tried to make the most of my weekend. I went down to the beach and worked on my tan for a few hours. I came back to my room to shower and got ready for the dance. The walk to the dance would have sucked if I wasn't so excited to see Alex.

I walked across the ballroom floor and my eyes fixed on Alex. When I reached the front stage, not one of my dance friends was there.

Alex looked down and saw me. I went on stage and asked, "Where is everyone?" He asked me why I didn't tell him I was coming down and I told him that I wasn't sure myself.

"I can't believe none of my friends are here. Doesn't matter…I came down to be with you. Can I stay with you tonight?"

Alex said he wished I would have told him I was coming down. He would have let me know that he had to leave to go back to Philly right after the dance for a family function the next day.

In my mind, insecurities were stirring. I thought to myself, "Sure, you have a family affair tomorrow, you probably have another date set up. I showed up and now you're squirming out of this the best way you can."

This is from the mind of a young woman whose two previous "nobody" boyfriends cheated on her and is now seeing a "somebody" who can see whoever he wants at the snap of a finger. Just then he totally redeemed himself by asking if I wanted to ride back home with him that night.

I did want to but I had no way to contact Danny to tell him I was leaving. After the way Ellen acted the first night I spent with Alex, I started to take other people's feelings into consideration. I didn't think that it was fair to Danny.

Besides that I hated myself for my immediate suspicion of Alex. That is the way crazy girls act. I wasn't crazy.

I told Alex that I could not leave that night. I asked if he could stop by my hotel for a little while.

He said he didn't know and that if he was not at the hotel by midnight, he wouldn't be coming.

I walked back to the hotel and sat on the porch waiting until 1AM.

I knew he was not coming. I felt so sad and lonely because what was going to be a great weekend turned out to be the worst. I could not wait to start packing for home.

Danny picked me up at noon and I never let on that I had a bad weekend, not even to Ellen.

I don't know why I didn't trust Alex. I think it was

the fact that girls just flung themselves on him. Why shouldn't he take advantage of them? Not once did he disrespect me. He never flirted or talked to other girls when I was around. He was nothing but sweet to me, always. I was confident, but the insecurity still lingered. That was my problem.

In a conversation one night on the phone with Alex, he asked my nationality. I told him I was half Italian. He wanted to know which of my parents was Italian. I told him it was my mother.

"Can she cook good?" he asked, "Does she make homemade spaghetti sauce?" Then went on and on about how much he loved pasta and homemade sauce. I got the hint and asked him if he would like to come for dinner some night? He said, "Sure would!" so I asked him if he could make it on a Tuesday. He accepted.

I went to work at the factory and hurried home to shower and change. I asked Mom if she needed any help and she said everything was almost ready. I went out on the porch and waited for Alex. He was right on time.

He smiled as he walked up the steps to the porch. I hugged and kissed him and we went inside. I introduced Alex to my dad. They shook hands, then to my mom who was putting food on the table.

We ate and had good conversation. Something Alex was not, was shy. He was great with people. He had to be because of the line of work he was in.

After dinner, Alex asked if we could watch the news on TV. Dad said he would help Mom clean up while I entertained Alex. I sat on the end of the couch and Alex took off his shoes. He laid on the couch putting his head on my lap.

When my Father came in the living room the darting death ray look my father gave me would have been enough to scare the birds from the trees!

My dad was "old school" and didn't approve of public displays of affection. His logic was, "If a guy does that in front of me, what does he do when I'm not around?"

That logic would prove sound because if Dad had only known what we'd already done, I don't think this couch thing would matter too much. I was still his little girl, and always will be. He always called me his "Little Dolly."

The other problem was that Dad saw Alex as more a man compared to the other guys I'd dated in the past.

After the TV news was over Alex asked me to go out with him to have ice cream. I really couldn't eat another thing but I said I would go anyway.

Alex thanked Mom for a great dinner and shook my dad's hand again.

We drove to Alex's neighborhood in Rhawnhurst. I had no idea he lived so incredibly close to me all these years. Why hadn't I seen him anywhere before? It was mind-boggling!

Alex got his ice cream and we walked on Bustleton Avenue for a while. We went for a drive and stopped for some heavy making out. We went to a small soda shop where we talked some more. I told him that I was a bridesmaid in my girlfriend Jenny's wedding. "It's in two weeks, will you be my date?" I blurted.

When I told him the exact date, he said that he had a gig that night and didn't think he could make it but he would try. He said if he was not there by 7:30, he wouldn't be making it at all.

I suggested that maybe he come by afterwards, and we could spend some time together. He told me he would try. That was one thing of many that I loved about him: he told it like it was and never led me on.

He drove me home. As we sat out in the car in front of my house, I hugged and kissed him some more. I never wanted to let him go, but it was a weeknight and I had work in the morning and the dress fitting the next night.

My hair was a light blonde at the time and I would occasionally tone down the color with a rinse called "Bashful Blonde".

On this night, when it dried, it turned my hair lavender! And what made it worst was, Jenny was having a "rainbow wedding." That is when every bridesmaid wears a different colored dress, and the color I picked was lavender. My hair was now the same color as the dress. Not what I had planned but it was too late that night to fix it.

I went to work the next day with lavender hair. Lavender hair is accepted now but I got quite a few stares back then. I had just enough time to rush home and eat dinner before Jenny was picking me up for the fitting.

When I tried on the dress my hair looked even more hideous. The seamstress at the store thought I did it intentionally. I reassured Jenny that my hair would not be this color for her wedding and she shouldn't worry.

Jenny couldn't have had a more beautiful day for her wedding and everything was going great.

The reception was in the evening, and at 7 o'clock I went outside to wait for Alex. I only waited until 7:30 and went back to the party.

Maybe he would be waiting for me when the reception was over and we could spend some time together but there was no sign of him and I won't lie, I was a bit disappointed even though he never made me promises.

Mid-week, Alex called and told me that he was going back down the shore for a few weeks to meet with some people about getting a new dance started. He asked if Ellen and I would be there.

I told him I wouldn't miss it. He called about two weeks later and said that it was all set up, and it was going to be in an old church. He gave me the directions and I wrote them down.

Ellen would find it. I don't know how, but she could find her way anywhere. I think she had a built in compass.

It was Labor Day weekend, the unofficial last weekend of summer. Ellen was not able to leave on Friday night like we always did, so we caught the bus on Saturday around 7 PM. By the time we checked into our room the dance at the ballroom was almost over so Ellen and I walked the boards and rode some amusements before calling it a night. It just felt good to be away from home.

Missing the dance on Saturday wasn't too bad since we were planning to go to Alex's new dance on Sunday night. Alex was probably thinking that I wasn't coming down because I was a no show at the ballroom.

Sunday was a beach day and after dinner we changed clothes and started walking to find this church. We came right to it after a fifteen-minute walk. Alex was set up at the first table by the door. "Sit down here," he said, "I have a few more things to take care of." As I sat, I began looking around the room to see who was there.

I saw a girl from the dance at "the rink." She always stared at me. I think she was jealous of me. I know she didn't like me, but on this night she was with my ex, Joe. I was 80 miles from home and haunted by jealous skating rink girl AND my ex boyfriend. They both kept looking at me making sure I saw them. The games people play. I saw them all right but I paid them no mind.

Alex was so happy to see me, he hugged me and whispered in my ear, "walk around to the back. I'll be back there in a couple seconds."

I began walking down a dark, long hallway. There were small rooms on each side. Every wall was painted black, with neon, day-glow orange, green and yellow peace sign paintings along with lots of "hippie" sayings. It was psychedelic.

Just then Alex came in view from the other end of the hall, "Here I am," he said.

He picked me up in his arms and swung me around. "I missed you!" he said, "I'm so glad you came," and we started kissing.

Oh, how I missed him too and we started to get a bit carried away. His hand slid up my skirt and he began tugging at my panties.

"No, not here!" I said. He assured me that no one would come back but I didn't feel comfortable doing anything there. I assured him there was no rush and asked him if he wanted me to spend the night with him.

He looked at me and said, "what do you think?"

Always respectable, he told me to go out first, so I turned and came out the way I went in. Alex went out the other side and we met back at the front table and smiled at each other.

Ellen asked where I was and I told her I was in the ladies' room.

Again with the look, "okay, and I am the Queen of England!" I told Ellen that I was spending the night with Alex and she said that was fine as long as she knew where I was.

All through the night, my ex and that girl, June, (that was what I think I heard someone call her) were getting cozy. They kept glancing over at me. I think she was hoping I was getting angry because she knew that he used to be my boyfriend. The one I think was getting angry though, was Joe. He couldn't help watching me and Alex dancing, laughing, and fooling around.

After the dance was over, Alex carried his equipment to the car that was parked out front.

Joe and June were standing on the front steps together. When Ellen and I came out we walked right over to Alex's car. The top was down so we hopped in. Right before pulling away I turned and looked June right in the eye. I gave her a look that said, "I have prime rib, and you have my moldy old Salisbury steak TV dinner!"

We dropped off Ellen at The Dixon, and went back to Alex's place where we made love again. We slept the night in each other's arms.

The next morning I laid in bed while Alex took a shower, thinking of how much I cared for him. Yes, I was in love, that I was sure of, but I didn't think Alex felt the same.

Did I want him to come back into the room swoop me up in his arms and say to me, "Sarah, you have been the girl I have been looking for all of my life and that I love you and I am never going to let you go?"

Um…well, yeah! But I knew down deep that was not going to happen. For me it was never about what I was to him…it was always about what he was to me.

Sure, I knew he enjoyed my company and he was always kind and sweet to me but that only made me want him more. I also felt extremely blessed and lucky that I was getting to have this time with him.

Summer was coming to an end and I wondered if we would still see each other or if it was just one of those summer flings?

I would find out soon enough.

September rolled around and life went back to normal. Work during the week and going to the dances on the weekend.

Alex had called a few times, but I was out dancing

or shopping and I still never felt comfortable returning his calls. After a month of not being able to reach me, the phone calls stopped. At first I was sad, but then just figured he found someone else or, he was maybe thinking the same about me.

It wasn't until one crisp fall Sunday night in November. Ellen and I were waiting in line to get tickets into the dance at the rink.

I was wearing a mustard gold color sweater with a navy blue wool pleated skirt, navy blue opaque tights and a pair of navy blue platform shoes with the stacked heels. Keeping me warm was my dark blue quilted mandarin collar jacket. I wore my hair down because it behaved much better when the weather was cool and dry.

A girl tapped me on the arm and asked if my name was Sarah? I told her it was and asked why? She said, "That guy over there is calling you."

I turned to see Alex waving me over in his car. I asked Ellen to get my ticket for me, and then I walked over to see him. My heart was beating wildly with excitement as I leaned into the window.

He said, "Hi, I called your house and your mom said that you went to the dance. You're not going in there are you?"

I said I was because for some odd reason I wanted to go to the dance more than be alone with him on that night. I still can't explain it.

He said, "I'm on my way to my sister's house to babysit. Why don't you come along and keep me company."

I was torn and I shouldn't have been. After all, this was yet another chance to be with him. I was flattered to death that he had come looking for me but if another minute had passed, I would have been inside and never would have known he had come looking for me at all.

I said "Okay. Maybe for an hour or so." I turned to see Ellen who was standing with her now boyfriend, Frank. I yelled to her that I would be back before the dance was over.

The kids were asleep upstairs when we got to Alex's sister's place. His sister and her husband left, leaving Alex and I alone in the living room. We talked a bit as I sat on his lap. It wasn't long before we were in his sister's bedroom making love again.

How I had missed him and why I didn't stay there with him for the rest of the night, I'll never know.

I told him that I had to get back or I would miss my ride home, and I left.

The dance had another half an hour before it was over. Ellen told me that she was going home with Frank. They couldn't take me home, so I took the bus home alone.

I know I hurt Alex's feelings a little. I don't know why I did these stupid things. Over and over I would make stupid choices when being with Alex was, I thought, everything to me.

He never called after that night and I pretty much gave up on ever seeing him again. I refused to get hurt by it all. Nothing could get through my protective shell and I knew that night was the last time I would see Alex, instead I chose to think that it was great while it lasted.

I would think about Alex more than I realized. I would always catch myself looking at our picture. I would get really angry with myself.

Why didn't I pursue him, call him, or invite him to dinner? Why didn't I show him I cared? If he would only call me again, I promised things would be different.

By March 1969, I was still dancing on the weekends and working Monday through Friday. Ellen and I were still the best of friends. Life went on and two other friends of ours began going to the dances with us.

A girl named Cassie who worked with Ellen and I at the factory, and one of Ellen's childhood friends named Dana.

Cassie was a heavyset girl with short black hair and Dana was a small-framed girl with long brown hair. She was quiet and shy.

We would find out much later that Cassie would also play the jealousy card.

It was Sunday at "the rink". Ellen and I were coming from the lady's room. I walked passed a guy sitting next to the pinball machine and after passing him I grabbed Ellen by the arm and said, "Did you see that guy? He looks just like Mick Jagger!"

Ellen didn't know which guy I was talking about, "Where?" she asked.

I had been crazy for Mick Jagger for years and I always loved the Rolling Stones. I had every one of their albums. Pictures and posters of Mick were pinned up all over my room.

Ellen finally saw him and said, "well, go get it girl!"

I planned to walk past him to see if he would notice me. Plan executed and then I looked over at Ellen, she shook her head "no."

I walked back again, this time I pretended that something was wrong with my shoe and stopped in front of him to fix it. When I got back to Ellen I asked if he looked? She said he didn't.

I observed him for a few more minutes. He looked as though he would rather be gouging out his own eyeballs with a plastic fork, than to be sitting there. His demeanor was miserable. But hey, he looked like Mick Jagger! I decided he was worth the work.

Ellen said, "Go ask him for a light!"

"And then what?" I asked.

"Just start talking. You're not new to this."

But the truth was I was a little scared and Ellen saw my fear. At that moment, she looked at me and said, "well if you don't, I will!"

"No, no. I'm going," I said. With the way he looked, I thought he might just tell me to leave him alone or worse, "get lost!"

As I approached him I was shaky and needed another minute.

His blond hair and the way he squinted his eyes whenever he took a drag from his cigarette gave him a bad boy, sexy look. That and his olive colored skin was making it all worth it.

"Got a light?" I asked.

He reached in his pocket for his lighter and lit my cigarette.

I continued, "Thanks. I don't think I have seen you here before. Is this your first time?"

He said it wasn't his first time and that he would only come there once in a while with his friends who played the pinball machine.

I asked him why he was sitting in the back. Then I asked him if he danced?

He seemed a little shy or backwards when he said he didn't want to dance and I couldn't figure him out but his sexy looks had me mesmerized! Don't forget, he looked like Mick Jagger!

"Well," I said, "I guess I'll see you around." And he answered with a simple, "yea, see ya."

I walked back to where Ellen was standing, and she asked if he was interested.

I simply replied, "The ball is in his court".

When the dance was over, he came over to me and asked if I would be there next week? I told him I was there every week.

It was a usual week at home and work as Sunday night rolled around again.

When I walked into the dance, I saw him, again sitting on the bench by the pinball machine. I walked around the other way and made sure not to pass him because I wanted him to find me.

Ellen and I went up front on the dance floor and talked to our friends. We danced a few dances and when I looked up, he was standing by the rails calling to me. I walked over and he said, "I saw you up here, I guess you didn't see me?"

Again, I was playing my little games to see if he was interested in me. If he never came up front I wouldn't have bothered him again, but the fact that he did, showed me he was interested. "Can we go sit in the back and talk?" he asked. "Sure" I said.

He said his name was Ken and I told him mine. He bought us both a soda and sat next to me as we talked for a while getting to know each other.

He was Italian. A blonde Italian! That would explain that great olive complexion and why he looked tan all the time.

When he smiled, and it didn't happen often, it made him look even sexier! I liked him but there was just something strange about him.

He didn't seem happy. Maybe his family life sucked. Who knows?

I gave him my phone number and he asked me if I wanted to go to the movies next Friday night? I said that I would.

Ken came to pick me up for the drive-in movie. It was a warm clear night and the drive-in was packed. "The Girl Can't Help It" was the main feature.

We both jumped in the back seat of the car to where we did some heavy making out but stopped just short of intercourse. He was okay with what we were already doing.

He was a good kisser too, but would sometimes zone out a bit when Jayne Mansfield would be on the movie screen taking her top off. It didn't bother me. After all, it was Jayne Mansfield!

He drove me home and before I got out of the car I asked him if I would see him Sunday night at the dance?

He said he hated that place and I asked him why he went then. Simply put, he said there is nothing else to do!

I wasn't missing my Sunday night dance so I said "well, I'll be there. If you're there, I'll see you and if not, I won't."

When I first got to the dance on Sunday night, I didn't see Ken and I figured he just didn't show. After about fifteen minutes, there he was, back standing by the rails looking for me.

I walked over. "Ah. I see you made it."

He said "yea, but I hate it!" and after a few songs he said, "I got to get out of here! Are you coming?"

"Where are we going?" I asked, and he said, "I don't know. Maybe sit in the car or something."

We walked to the corner lot where he was parked.

As we sat, he seemed to become agitated. I couldn't even talk to him. There was no conversation at all and I could hardly breathe with all of the smoke building up inside the car. The heat was on and I was getting a headache.

I said "well look, you're clearly in a mood, so I'm going back into the dance." He said, "I might be here when you come out, I don't know." He was gone when the dance was over.

The next night Ken called and said he was sorry, he was just in a bad mood and should not have come at all. I forgave him and the next week after the dance we all piled in Ellen's boyfriend's car.

Frank headed up to the drive-thru for something to eat. On the way, I stuck my head out the window and screamed, "hi!" to Jenny, who was probably getting home from work.

I pulled myself back into the car and Ken said, "You know that blimp?" and Ellen struck back as she was good at doing, "That's not nice," but Ken just snickered.

I was so embarrassed for him, but he just seemed like he enjoyed getting a rise out of people. He didn't even know my friends so how could he say things like that! After that night I didn't see him again and he stopped coming to the dances.

Within weeks of that awful night, I began dating a guy who was one of our friends from the dance. His name was Bill. He was tall, thin and had reddish blond hair. He was also a good dancer, which was always a plus with me.

On a Saturday night at one of the fire hall dances, I was off to the side of the stage dancing with Bill when suddenly my ex, Joe was standing next to me. He had been drinking.

He leaned in and said in my ear, "you know you can never find anyone else that can make love to you like I can!" I pulled away and smiled, he said, "you know it. Come on, admit it."

I thought, "you poor sap, who are you trying to convince, yourself or me?"

He said, "anytime you want me, you just let me know." He only wanted me because I was seeing Bill.

It wasn't long before I found out that Bill was taking drugs and we broke up.

☆

Summer of 69 was coming and I was looking forward to great times at the shore again.

We headed down on the third week of June for a weekend and to make our reservations for our mandatory vacation at the factory. We loved The Dixon and wanted to stay there in July.

I was wondering if Alex would still be running the dance and what, if anything would happen between us.

Saturday night came none too soon for me. As I entered the ballroom, my heart felt like it was going to leap out of my chest. As I walked across the dance floor, my eyes immediately went to the stage.

He was there. I was so happy to see him again. I walked up and stood under where he was standing on stage. He looked down and exclaimed, "Sarah!" as he jumped from the stage, down to the dance floor and hugged me. "I'm so glad to see you!"

"You are?" I said, but in mind I was thinking, "what happened to the phone calls, and the six months of not hearing from you?"

I kept those questions to myself, never saying it. After all, it was not like we were going steady or anything like that. I didn't feel I had the right to cross-examine him so I just smiled.

"Still got those cute little dimples I see. What are you doing after the dance?"

I wanted to be with him again because all that love was still there. He had such a powerful hold on me, and I was just putty in his hands. That great feeling was coming back fast and furious like nothing had ever changed.

After the dance I did leave with Alex. We went to a diner then back to his place.

He said, "wow your hair got long since I saw you last."

I told him that it was a fall (a hair piece of long hair that was very popular in the sixties).

"Are you kidding me?" he said shocked.

I said, "No, see?" and I took the fall off.

He said "a guy can't tell what's real on you girls anymore."

I didn't bother to ask him what he meant by that because it didn't matter now. I was with the man I loved once more, and once more we made love.

After saying goodnight he fell asleep fast but I always would lay awake for a while looking out the window.

I could see flashes of lighting, and rumbles of distant thunder. There was a storm approaching and I could smell the cool rain as it hit the steamy hot sidewalks.

I always loved storms. There is that sense of danger and it made my pulse race but at the same time it gave me the warm fuzzies.

There was something special about this night aside from being with Alex again, a feeling of familiarity.

Making love with Alex was getting better and better as we were getting to know one another's bodies, our likes and dislikes.

Just being in that room, a room that was no different than any other rented room at the shore, but this was his room.

We shared other nights there together but this one was perfect and I was lulled to sleep by gently falling rain.

The next morning I quietly crept out of bed and used the bathroom, fixed my hair and touched up my makeup. I put my clothes on and climbed back in bed with Alex. He was sound asleep and I was wide-awake. I knew our ride back to the city was leaving earlier than usual and I still had to pack, so I nudged him.

He woke up and gave me a big kiss. I explained that I had to meet Ellen early. We decided to skip breakfast and he drove me back to The Dixon.

We said our goodbyes and not long after, Ellen and I were on the road heading back to Philly.

Back home and back to work, my weeks went on as usual.

I knew I was getting ready to have my period because I was crampy and bloated, but it never came.

One Sunday night after the dance, a bunch of us piled in Frank's car and headed up to the burger take-out. We parked in the parking lot and one of the guys was asking everyone what they wanted. I don't know if it was the mention of food or the smell of burgers wafting in the air but suddenly, I felt nauseated.

I asked for someone to open the back door because I thought I was going to be sick. I got out and walked behind the car and stood for a minute. The sick feeling subsided.

When I got back into the car I was hungry but I didn't get to order any food so I just took a bite of Ellen's burger.

Later that night, while lying in bed, I began to fear the worst. I was now four weeks late for my period. Could I be feeling sick already? Ellen knew I was late but I think neither one of us wanted to realize the possibility.

When planning another weekend at the shore, I declined because I feared getting sick and having everyone assume what was wrong with me so I stayed close to home. I had Ellen swear she would not say anything to Alex and I trusted her to keep my secret until I found out for sure.

Ellen took Dana with her to the shore. I didn't ask if they had fun when they came home I only asked if Alex had asked for me. Ellen said, "yes I told him something came up and you couldn't come down. He said he would call you."

Alex did call and asked me if everything was all right. I said yes and told him it was just a family function I had to attend.

I went to see a doctor the third week in August and he confirmed my fears. I was going to have a baby, Alex's baby.

I confided in my mother, who was not happy with the news. We both didn't want to face the wrath of my father. After all, I never wanted my dad to think badly of me and I think that was the hardest part of all.

My mother broke the news to my dad and all he would say to me was "what's your husband's name Sarah? What's your husband's name Sarah?"

I finally said, "he is not my husband." And from

that day, no one ever asked about the father of my baby.

I had Mom continue to screen my calls from Alex. She would tell him I wasn't home. He would eventually stop calling the house.

I couldn't tell him I was pregnant. His career was really taking off and I didn't want to hit him with this. Besides, I couldn't stand to live if he got mad or hated me in any way! I would rather die so I selfishly gave him up as not to mess up his life in any way.

If I thought for one minute he loved me it would have been different.

So I would put my love for Alex, like a trophy I had won on a shelf, in the attic of my mind and my heart, and went on with my life once again.

I was going to be a mother and that was my priority. That was my focus.

As I began to show, everyone I worked with soon knew I was expecting and once everyone knew it wasn't so bad. No one treated me any different; in fact, they were nicer and much concerned for my well being.

It was the shame my father instilled in me that made me uncomfortable and uneasy. I believed that my father was ashamed of what people thought of him. It was just a feeling at first but after awhile he got use to the way it was.

My friendship with Ellen was still strong, but I was not going out much and quickly becoming a homebody.

Ellen was going out and hanging around with Dana and Cassie. She was chummier with Cassie and Ellen started seeing a new guy that worked with us at the factory named Ray.

Morning sickness came anytime it wanted to, in the morning, noon or night, and it plagued me for nearly five months.

Every morning when I would get off the bus at work, I would need to sit on a nearby step until the sick feeling passed. I never vomited but the feeling never missed a day.

Out of the blue, I got a call one night from Ken. He asked if he could come over to see me. I really had no interest in getting involved with him again but I said he could visit.

When he came over we sat outside on the steps in front of my house.

He began to tell me that he was leaving in a few days for the Army, and asked if I would write to him. He seemed like he needed a friend and I guess I did too so I said "sure." What harm could it do?

I did tell him I was pregnant and he was supportive. He assured me that everything would be okay, I shouldn't worry and that I was going to make a great mom.

Talking to him that night was like talking to someone else, not the Ken who embarrassed me that night in the back of Frank's car.

This Ken was sweet and caring. I thought maybe the Army would straighten him out. Time would tell. He gave me a kiss and a hug goodbye and I wished him good luck.

About three weeks later I got a letter from Ken. He always asked how I was feeling and I looked forward to his letters. I knew there would never be anything romantic about our relationship. I think we were doing much better as friends.

After boot camp, Ken was on leave and came to see me; I was going into my fifth month of pregnancy. We sat there and talked for a while when he said he was being sent to Korea for six months or more and again I promised him I would write. About once a month I would get a letter from him, and sometimes I would make and send him homemade cookies or banana nut bread.

He would write back saying that he shared the treats with the other guys, and that everything was good! He asked me to keep them coming. They just didn't get treats like that from the Army.

In one of the letters he sent me, he included a picture of him with one of his buddies and in return I sent him one of me.

We wrote back and forth the whole time he was away. It was nice getting his letters all during my pregnancy.

I received a welcome call from Jenny. We had not talked for a while.

I told her I was having a baby and she, like always, was there to jump in and be my friend.

Her husband was going on a trip for work and would be gone for a few days and Jenny asked me if I would like to come and stay with her, get out of the house for a little and she said she would enjoy the company.

I hesitated at first but Jenny said, "come on. It will

be fun, like when we were kids."

I said okay and by mid-afternoon on Friday, Jenny picked me up. This was the first time seeing her new house.

We talked, stayed up late, looked at pictures and ate ice cream but after two days I wanted to go home because I felt sad and lonely. I guess maybe it was hormones.

Weeks later Jenny called again, this time with sad news. She told me her dad had passed away. I told her that I wanted to come to the funeral.

She said, "I knew you would, so I waited until it was all over to tell you. Trust me Sarah, my dad was unrecognizable and I didn't want you seeing him like that in your condition."

He had died of bone cancer and I can always remember him being sick.

Whenever I would be over Jenny and Amy's house he would be in the bathroom vomiting on a daily basis. I suppose he was sick for many years, but when he felt well enough he was a lot of fun. Always dancing at countless wedding receptions. I think he was a hard drinking Irish man but he was always nice to me and the family always treated me like one of their own.

I continued working until February. I was due on March 9th. My neighbor next door threw me a baby shower. I got a second hand crib and everything I needed. Ellen brought her new friend Cassie and surprised me with a playpen.

Late in the morning of March 11th, I was taken to the hospital to have my baby. I was scared. I was lonely and I did not know what to expect. The nurses told me it was completely normal for all first time mothers to have those feelings.

I was not really in labor yet, but past my due date so they kept me for a while. By 5 PM that afternoon, I was starting to have pains. I can only remember being on a gurney in the hallway, and grabbing a nurse's arm until the pain subsided. She stood there until I let go of her.

I knew my water broke and that I was having my baby soon. That's all I could recall until I was wheeled into a dark room. All I could see was a small orange light just like the little orange dot from Bible camp. I remembered the nurse wheeling me in said to my roommates, "put out that cigarette and get to sleep!"

When the nurse left the room, I heard a voice say to me, "we have been wondering how long it would be before they brought you in here. It's about time!" and with that, sluggish and exhausted, I fell asleep.

The next morning the other two girls in the room introduced themselves to me. We all had baby girls. The nurse brought the babies in one by one.

She handed me a baby that I had never seen. It was 1:42 AM and I guess that was too late for them to show me my child.

I do know this…when I looked at the baby, there was nothing. I had no feelings at all. Aren't you supposed to instantly love your baby? Feel some kind of connection to her? What kind of mother was I? I looked at the armband, and the last name was not mine.

I rang for the nurse and questioned her about it. She apologized and explained that another woman was supposed to give birth before me, and I was in her bed. When I gave birth first, they put me in that bed. She apologized again. Then she went to go get my baby.

Sweet relief! But, for real? I mean, how many

times do you hear that happening? When she brought in my daughter, I said to myself, "this was more like it!"

She was like a little doll and I loved her immediately. I named her Kimberly. Her twinkling little eyes gazed at me in wonder as she wrapped her little fingers around one of mine. When she was just born, she did not resemble Alex or myself, but as she grew, there were times I could plainly see Alex.

Ellen was spending more time with Cassie and only stopped by on occasion. Something fishy was going on.

I suspected they were dabbling in drugs but I never said a word to Ellen. Besides, she thought I didn't know what was going on. I figured it was marijuana or pills. I noticed Ellen losing weight rapidly and she was dressing like a hippie.

Our lives were going in different directions but I still loved her and asked her to be Godmother to my child. She was thrilled and said yes.

Danny, who drove me down the shore that horrible weekend I was alone, was going to be the Godfather.

After six weeks, I went back to work at the factory. I continued living at my parent's house so my mother would watch Kim for me.

It took awhile for me to feel myself again. Having a baby took a lot out of me and for months I felt weak.

During this time, it was now obvious Ellen was doing drugs with Cassie, and was serious with Ray, her boyfriend.

Aside from her weight loss, I did not see much change in her but our boss did. He told Ellen and Ray that he no longer wanted them working there. He suggested that they get some help.

Ellen came onto the floor and told me that her and Ray just got fired. I didn't ask why because she still believed that I didn't know about the drug use.

Maybe I should have intervened but I did not want to embarrass her.

Ellen and I didn't see each other for months, until one day she came by my house with a new man named Jack. He was very tall, thin and obviously a drug addict too.

My mother did not pass judgment. My father on the other hand could not hide his disapproval; although he did not say anything, I could tell he did not like Jack.

When she said she was with someone new, I was hopeful. And now that I met him, I was crushed. I knew being with this guy was not going to turn her around.

Close to a year after that visit, I received a picture of her new son and a letter telling me that she was still with Jack. That was the last time I heard from her.

Our lives were now in two different places. Our friendship had always been based on similar interests like dancing and fashion. I was knee deep in diapers and she was doing drugs. I couldn't imagine her having a baby with Jack. Maybe they cleaned up their act after her son was born. I prayed that was the case.

I missed her very much. From time to time, I

would take out my pictures of her and Alex, and always hoped that one day I would get a call or visit out of the blue.

After all, she knew where to find me. I had no idea where she was now.

PART THREE

Where Does My Heart Belong?

When it got busy at the factory, they would hire more girls, and one of the new girls named Karen instantly became my friend. We were not as close as Ellen and I were, but we were friends just the same.

Karen was a pretty girl with long golden blonde, wavy hair. She had a pretty smile.

Another girl we worked with asked us if we wanted to go to this new club that just opened called "The Scene." The following Sunday night we all went.

It was over a year and a half since I had been out dancing. Just the idea of getting dressed up and dancing again excited me beyond belief.

The Scene was a cool place. It had three bars on two levels with tables and chairs overlooking the dance floor.

There were lots of colored lights that pulsated to the sound of the music, strobe lights that made everyone look like they were moving in slow motion but the best feature of the place was the Lucite dance floor. Each square on the floor was lighted and changed colors to the beat of the music.

This was to become a common nightclub feature when disco kicked in. Remember it was only 1970 and this was wild and never seen before.

Karen and I started going every Sunday night.

I had, in the meantime, received a letter from Ken. He said he was coming home and wanted to get together. I told him about The Scene and where it was located and asked him to meet me there on Sunday night.

I told him that I would wait by the front door for him.

When Sunday night came, I told Karen to get a table and I would wait for Ken. When he got there he had a friend with him. His name was Roy and I introduced them both to Karen. We ordered drinks and Ken was babbling about how he couldn't find the place when the next words from his mouth were, "you got fat!"

"What?" I couldn't believe what I was hearing! True I had put on fifteen pounds of baby fat, but I was working hard to get it off and had already taken about six pounds off. How dare he?

I could not even speak at first, then I sprung like a coiled snake, "give me a break I just had a baby three months ago! The weight just doesn't fall off, you know!"

Karen said, "that's not very nice" before leaving to sit at the bar. Ken just sat there smirking.

I thought to myself that I didn't need this shit in my life. There was clearly something wrong with this guy. The Army didn't change him.

I told Ken that I had to use the bathroom. Instead I walked to the other side of the room and sat down at the bar with Karen.

I had no intentions of returning to that table again. I could see Ken and Roy sitting there for about ten minutes before he got the hint and left.

I never saw or heard from Ken again.

One night when leaving the club, Karen and I were walking across the parking lot to catch the bus for home. Karen and I would ride together to the bus depot, then she would get her bus and I would get mine. We came from opposite directions.

Thinking back in hindsight, makes me shiver to think how we traveled around late at night and all alone. True, it was a much different time back then. Not that we didn't meet up with the occasional pervert or weirdos who would masturbate in front of strangers.

On this night, there was a guy walking behind us. He asked where we were heading.

"To the bus stop," I said, and then he sat next to me on the step.

He began to only talk to me. He asked me what my name was. He said his name was Tom. He was kind of cute with longish black hair. He looked as if he wanted to be an Elvis Presley impersonator. He would have made a good one.

"Well my bus is coming," I said and as I was boarding the bus he asked if he could call me. I said it would be okay and rattled off my number so fast, that once on the bus I said to Karen, "he'll never remember that number."

I was wrong and the next night he called. We talked and he told me that he worked at a well known department store in town as a shoe salesman. After a little while I told him I had to go. He asked if he would see me at the club on Sunday and I answered, "most likely."

When Sunday came, Tom never showed up and to tell you the truth, I was glad. I just wanted to dance with Karen and have fun. When I gave Tom my number, I was hoping he would not remember it.

I just wasn't sure how I felt about him. The next night Tom called again and said he was sorry but some family thing happened or something like that. I really didn't care.

Then he asked me if I would go out with him on Saturday night, and I agreed. He asked me if I would mind coming into town to meet him, because he would be working until five.

On Saturday, I arrived at the store at 4:45. He came out and handed me a huge box, "this is for you."

It was a great pair of boots. "Try them on, see if I have the size right." They were a perfect fit. I thanked him and told him they were just fine.

We walked to a restaurant a few blocks from his work and had dinner, and then we rode the bus home. It was a good date, but still, I wasn't sure of my feelings for him.

As the weeks went on, he was charming me, and told me that the night he saw me walking across the parking lot, he told his friend, "that's the girl I'm going to marry."

Tom and I began to go steady, and by this time Karen was getting married soon and not going to The Scene much, so I would go alone and meet Tom there.

He worked as a bartender on Sunday nights, and with Tom not being a dancer, my Sunday nights consisted of me sitting on a bar stool, watching Tom serve drinks.

It killed me to not be out on the floor dancing but after three months of this torture, the club suffered a fire, and was never rebuilt.

There were times Tom and I got along good and other times not so good. We would make dates to go out but he stood me up a lot.

Once on my birthday, he planned to take me to this expensive and "high class" place in Center City Philadelphia. I was dressed to the nines, and he never showed up.

He called the next day with some story about his sister's refrigerator breaking down and all of the food went bad. How her kids were all hungry and he had to help her.

I was furious! It was always some crappy story.

He would often borrow money from me and never pay all of it back. I don't know why I put up with it. I guess I was falling in love with him.

Like I said, there were good times, but I was to discover that he was a drinker, and a mean drinker at that.

Every time we went to a party or a wedding we would fight. The night always ended with him dropping me off and me throwing a slab of wedding cake at the back of his car as he sped away. The next day all would be forgiven.

I can recall one night, we were driving home from a party and he was being his drunken, nasty self. He had sped right through a stop sign and when we got to my house, a cop car was behind us.

The policeman got out of his patrol car, the lights reflecting off of my parent's house. He immediately noticed that Tom had been drinking and told him that he would not be doing any more driving on that night.

The cop asked me if Tom could spend the night at my house to which I answered, "No! Not the way he was treating me all night. I don't care what happens to him!"

The officer ended up driving him home instead of arresting him for drunk driving.

Despite all of this, Tom and I got engaged.

I thought that marriage would make him grow up. That having a wife and a child depending on him would give him a sense of responsibility. I felt that I was ready for marriage. I know now that he wasn't ready.

Along with his drinking and abuse, someone should have stopped us from getting married solely on the fact that he never had money and what money he did make, it wasn't enough to start a family.

Tom would attempt to make a difference without trying too hard. He started a new job working for the city's transit company. He got the job easily because his father was a head honcho, high atop the ladder.

The terminal he worked out of was close to where I worked at the factory so every day Tom would pick me up and drive me home.

Friday nights were the worst. I would always be left waiting and he would never show up for our dates.

When Tom would get his paycheck each week, he would cash it immediately and go out and get drunk with the guys from work.

Tom didn't attempt to bond with my daughter either. She would come out with us only once in awhile. The rest of the times, my parents would watch her.

In a conversation one day, I told him that I used to date Alex Bentley before I met him. He became jealous and although he never asked me who Kim's dad was, the thought that Kim could have been Alex's child made him loathe him even more.

As time went on, I put up with Tom and his careless, selfish antics. Always feeling like I was being taken for granted.

There was always someone more important than me. He jumped at invitations by others using me as a last resort.

My biggest competition for his time and attention was his father. He idolized his father and wanted to be just like him in every way.

His mother died when he was nine months old so I don't think that he was ever taught about love. His grandmother raised him and he adored her too but I didn't feel like I had to compete with her as much.

His father remarried, but his stepmother was mean to him and his siblings. I didn't realize my mother-in-law had the puzzle solved.

If I had known that being mean and unaffectionate would have won me the love of my husband, I never would have married him. I was never mean or unaffectionate.

Tom would tell me he loved me, but how could he have? His actions spoke louder than words. But I chose to believe that he thought he loved me.

I had lots of other guys bidding for my time.

There was the guy who rode past me every morning on my walk to work. He would blow his horn, and wave to me and I would just smile and wave back.

This went on for two weeks until one morning he asked if I wanted a ride. I just thanked him and said "no."

There was the truck driver who picked up the goods at the factory. I would make sure I was there everyday to help him load his truck, and to flirt with him.

Then there was Neil who worked at the ARCO gas station across the street from the factory. Neil would often ask if I would like a ride home but I would turn him down. I was developing a serious crush on him.

He was good looking, with a medium build. Neil had thick, black curly hair that was always disheveled in the sexiest of ways.

I know he liked me and I knew I could have had him whenever I wanted but I just couldn't bring myself to cheat on Tom.

I loved the extra attention I was getting from these guys as it filled a void left by the lack of attention I was getting from Tom.

There was a small luncheonette around the corner from the factory, and everyone that worked close by would eat lunch there. In the morning it was the place to grab a fast cup of coffee.

Every morning I would buy my morning coffee and bagel, and place my lunch order for that afternoon.

On this day, when I stopped in to pick up my lunch, Jay, the owner, said it had been already paid for.

I asked him who paid for it and he said that a secret admirer paid. I wondered who that could be.

Jay said he couldn't tell me because he was sworn to secrecy.

I knew it must have been Neil. Should I thank him? What if it wasn't him? What if Tom stopped by and paid for it?

This went on for weeks and I was feeling a little guilty for not thanking someone, but who should I be thanking?

I asked Jay, "just tell me is it Neil?" and Jay said it wasn't Neil.

I had started noticing another guy, looking over at me when I was doing orders on the platform. He was standing there smiling at me while wiping his hand on a towel. I returned his smile.

He was a burly man, handsome and rugged looking.

He was not my type at all. Guys like this never appealed to me before but there was…something about him.

The next day I pointed him out to Jay and asked if he was the one buying my lunch. Jay said "yes, but you didn't hear it from me. His name is Robbie."

The next afternoon, after picking up lunch I walked over to Robbie as he was standing outside. All the guys from the gas station liked to watch the girls from the factory.

"Are you the one that's been paying for my lunch all of these weeks?"

He said he was and I thanked him. I said it was nice of him and I told him my name. He already knew.

"My name is Rob. Can I ask you a question?"

"Yes," and I wondered what that question could possibly be.

"Is that guy that picks you up every day your husband?" he asked.

"No, he is my fiancé," I answered apprehensively.

He told me that all the guys at the station thought I was the prettiest girl working over there.

And do you know what I said then? I said, "even Neil?"

He said, "yeah, even Neil."

Even though Robbie was cute, I was still crushing on Neil.

I had noticed that a week went by and I hadn't seen Neil. I asked Robbie where he was and he told me that he got fired.

Robbie looked at me and said "always questions about Neil. What about me?" and I answered, "I just haven't seen him, that's all."

It was Friday afternoon. I was done work, and stood up once more by Tom. It was Friday after all and Friday was payday.

Robbie was getting off work too and he saw me waiting, "need a ride?"

"I think so," I said, and he offered to drive me home.

We talked about nothing in particular. We kept it light and social but then he said that he felt like he had to let me know something about him.

"I'm married," he said and for some reason that didn't bother me in the least. After all, it was just a little crush he had on me, what harm could come from that?

I was home now and I thanked him for the ride. I told him I would see him on Monday and to my surprise, spent most of my weekend thinking about Robbie and looking forward to Monday.

Once again, it was the busy season at the factory, and we were all asked to work overtime, into the night, until 9 o'clock.

Only a few of us stayed and worked for the extra hours. We all ordered dinner and had it delivered. We ate outside on the factory steps.

The night air was hot and thick with humidity.

Robbie was just finishing up work and getting ready to leave when he walked over to ask if I needed a ride home.

I told him that Tom was picking me up later and thanked him for offering. In turn, I then asked him if he wanted a piece of my shrimp. He smiled real big and said, "is that all you're going to offer me?"

I gave him my shy but sexy look followed by a little giggle. He just laughed and said he would see me tomorrow.

Tom drove me home and wanted to come in. I told him I was really beat and just wanted to go right to bed, and that was exactly what I did.

I was so exhausted from the extra work and the extreme heat, but I would lay there in bed thinking of Robbie, and what happened tonight.

There was definitely sexual tension between Robbie and I. We both felt it and every day after that night, we would have our lunch break together, if you want to call it lunch. We would spend our hour parked behind the factory in Robbie's car, making out. My food always got cold so half of the time I didn't eat. Robbie was satisfying my appetite just fine. I was thin as it was, but was taking off more weight by skipping meals.

I was feeling guilty seeing Robbie and cheating on Tom. That was who I was, "Miss Always Do The Right Thing," so I broke it off with Tom and gave him back the ring and I felt much better.

Although I was having an affair with someone's husband, it was exciting to me and gave me a little rush even though it was wrong. Robbie was glad to hear that I broke it off and told me I was too good for that guy.

A month went by and I heard nothing from Tom. This was strange because he never gave up easy on me before. When we would fight, he would keep calling and coming around. I would tell him I didn't want to see him anymore, but he kept it up until he broke me down.

I was happy that Tom wasn't trying to get me back. Perhaps because of Robbie's size, Tom was a little intimidated.

I looked forward to my lunch times with Robbie and when he could drive me home from work.

One day Robbie told me that he would no longer be working at that Arco and that they were transferring him somewhere else.

I was upset, but he assured me that he would still be around for lunch when he could and that he still had to go to this station to get paid.

He kept his promise. He didn't come every day but he came often. I would go out on the platform to see if his car was out there five minutes before the lunch whistle blew and when it was, I would get excited.

Robbie called me late one Saturday afternoon and asked if I would like to take a ride to the Poconos with him and his buddy the next day. I said yes to his invite and on Sunday early afternoon they picked me up.

When I got in the car, Robbie's friend said, "how

the hell did you get a gorgeous girl like her?"

I thanked him for his compliment then he asked me what I saw in Robbie. He was just kidding, of course.

The ride was pleasant and relaxing. Robbie's friend left us off at Robbie's summer home and then went to visit a woman nearby that he was seeing. Robbie and I were alone for the first time since we got together and needless to say it wasn't long before we were in bed. It was freezing and there was no heat but Robbie found ways to make me forget about the cold.

I stopped him just short of intercourse. That would be all I needed. To get pregnant by a married man would surely put my father in an early grave.

Not as long as Robbie was married. He understood my apprehension and told me it was ok. He said, "You let me know when you're ready. It's up to you."

On the drive home, we stopped off to eat but I only had a soft drink because I wasn't hungry.

Robbie and I sat in the backseat and cuddled. Robbie's friend knew we didn't get time alone and he didn't seem to mind our public displays of affection. It was a great day we spent together.

A major public transit strike was underway. Without the bus, I couldn't get to work. A friend of Robbie's who worked around the corner from the gas station said that he would pick me up and take me to work since he went right past my house everyday. He would pick me up in the morning and take me home after work.

His name was John and he was a little on the short side, but he was still taller than me. He had long black hair, wore glasses and had one of those faces. You know the kind, you don't think he is that nice looking but the more you see him the better he looks. His looks were growing on me and he was a real nice guy. I appreciated the rides but at first it was a little awkward but after a few days we became friends.

It turned out to be a long strike with no end in sight and John was there on time, every day, without fail.

One day while driving home, John asked me to go to a concert with him, I was tempted just in a friendly way but declined. I didn't want him to get the wrong idea because it was clear John was falling for me.

The next day Robbie said that he could drive me home.

I asked him if he had told John. I insisted that we go around and let John know, so we went over together before leaving. When we got there, Robbie said, "wait here, I'll tell him," and as I watched them talking through the window it seemed as if they were arguing. I could hear their voices getting louder and I turned away. I was becoming a bit embarrassed because some how I got the feeling it was about me.

When Robbie came out he was angry. I asked what was wrong. He said, "I've had it with that guy. He pisses me off. He had a lot of nerve asking you out like that. He knows how I feel about you!"

I reassured him he had nothing to worry about, that I liked John as a friend and that's why I turned him down and I was just going to continue riding in with him to work.

I told Robbie that I cared too much for him.

He said "you don't know how much I wished I met you before I met my wife. Things would definitely be different because I think I'm falling in love with you."

Wow, how I loved hearing those words, but I knew deep down that he was never going to leave his wife, and I wasn't sure I wanted him to. I think this relationship was safe for me. I felt like it wasn't going much farther than this and that was okay.

I still hadn't heard anything from Tom. This really wasn't like him. He just wasn't known to give up a fight. I spoke too soon because one evening, he called me in a drunken stupor. He started rattling off that he knew about my married boyfriend, where he lived and, he knew more about Robbie than I did.

He had a cop friend of his run Robbie's license plate number through the system. It would seem that Tom had been stalking me and following us. Tom had also traded cars with a friend of his so I wouldn't know he was following us.

Tom was getting angry and was jealous of Robbie. I was correct in worrying about Tom's disappearance for so long. There wasn't anything I wouldn't put past Tom.

Tom started his frequent calls again. He continued to ask me for another chance, continued to ask if he could see me and I always told him "no."

The truth was, I was happy with Robbie and the way things were. Yes, I was falling hard for Robbie, he was kind and sweet and although he was big and masculine, he was just a big teddy bear.

One day sticks out in my mind. I was doing an order on the platform at work when I looked up and saw Robbie get out of his car with his wife. Knowing they were married and *seeing* they were married were two separate things. Seeing them together upset me so much. I turned, went back inside, and asked my friend Mary to finish the order for me so I wouldn't have to go back out there.

I went into the restroom, started shaking, and started to cry. I don't know why I was so emotional, but an hour later when work was over, Robbie was outside waiting for me.

I got in the car and he began apologizing, saying he had no choice and that they were in the neighborhood and needed gas. If he didn't get the gas at the station where he worked, his wife would have wondered.

"What could I do? I had to come back to see you. I knew you were upset and I couldn't go on vacation and leave you like that." And with that said, he grabbed me and gave me the most passionate kiss. It was the longest kiss I ever had laid on me.

That was the nicest thing anyone ever did for me and I knew then that he really did care about my feelings and me and I loved him even more for it.

Robbie and his wife went away on their vacation and I spent two boring weekends close to home. Those weekends made me anxious to get back to work.

When I got to work on Monday, Robbie was there waiting for me and he was angry. "what's wrong?" I asked.

He said, "I want you to tell your old boyfriend that when I see him, I'm going to kick his ass!" He proceeded to tell me that over the weekend, somebody drove by his house and "egged" it. "I know it was him and a few of his drunken buddies, so if you talk to him, you tell him what I said!"

When I did hear from Tom I told him exactly what Robbie said. Tom's response was, "tell him any time!" Tom talked big, but Robbie could kill Tom with one punch. I told Tom he was being childish, to grow up and, more importantly, to stop calling me.

Tom didn't do anything else to Robbie after that. I think he knew deep down that Robbie was not one to be messed with.

The whole situation of the last few weeks, seeing and falling for a married man, Tom calling all of the time, begging me to see him again, it was all starting to get to me.

My friend Mary at work asked me to bring Kim and come stay at her house in New Jersey during our mandatory week long vacation from work.

That week I used to look so forward to. That week I used to have amazing times dancing the night away and sunning on the beach. That week I used to spend with Ellen. That week I used to see Alex.

Now I hated that week.

I tried my hardest to start something new on my vacation. Do something new that would take my mind off of all my troubles.

Mary had a daughter Kim's age and I thought they would have a lot of fun together so I said "yes" to the invitation. It would be good for me to get away from everything for a while.

Kimberly and I took "The El" train to the 30th Street Station and then the train that went to New Jersey. Kim remembers this trip better than I do.

Mary had a friend of hers pick us up at the train station. When we arrived Mary and her mother who lived with her came out to greet us. Mary's daughter, Debbie came running from inside with their dog following behind and the kids started playing on the lawn. They were getting along nicely.

I couldn't believe what a long commute to work Mary had every day. I thought I had it bad taking one trolley.

She said it was about an hour and a half each way which I thought was ludicrous, but Mary had been working there long before me and was used to it I guess.

The house was a nice size with a huge yard in back.

After dinner we sat while the kids played.

Later that night, Mary showed Kim and me to our room and I remember there was a storm coming.

Kim and I sat by the window watching the lighting. It was putting on quite a show. Mary's house was more of a suburban house so there was plenty of sky between homes, not like the city where everything is tightly woven and close together.

The next day, we took the kids shopping at a strip mall. I bought some clothing for Kim and myself. When we came back to Mary's house we sat in the yard and relaxed and while doing so my thoughts drifted to Robbie and I was missing him a lot.

All of the sudden, Kim started sneezing uncontrollably. Her eyes were red, watering and swollen. Her nose was so stuffed up she could hardly breathe.

I told Mary that I thought that Kim was getting sick and maybe it would be a good idea if we went home. Mary said if we could stay the night, her husband would be home in the morning and would drive us all the way back.

I said okay. It was late and I didn't want to take her home sick on the train, the El, and then a trolley.

Kim was having such a good time, even though she didn't feel well, she wanted to stay, but I didn't want anyone to get sick. I did not know what was wrong with her.

The next morning after breakfast we started for home. When we got there, I thanked her husband for the ride and thanked Mary for taking us in. I was sorry we had to cut it short. I gave her a big hug and told her I'd see her at work on Monday.

After being home for an hour, Kim's symptoms cleared up like she was never sick. It was then, I figured it had to be an allergic reaction to the dog. Kim had never really been around a dog for that long before. I was relieved that in no time she was back to normal and she wasn't suffering anymore.

I still had a few days left to my week long vacation so Kim, my mother and I took the bus to a shopping center to start getting Kim's back to school clothes.

It was a hot and humid day. We were almost there but when we stood up to get off the bus, I began to feel strange and shaky and was perspiring profusely.

I told my mom that I didn't feel so good and we had better go into the restaurant and sit for a minute. Once inside the air conditioning, I felt refreshed, but I was still not feeling right.

I could see that Kim was getting upset, so I tried to assure her I was going to be fine, but I was having a hard time believing it myself.

I asked my mother to please get me a glass of water when she came back I could hardly drink it. I was shaking so much. My head hurt and I was breathing heavily. What seemed like hours were only minutes and soon I was fine.

My mother kept suggesting that it was the heat, and maybe we should go back home, but I felt better and chose to continue on our shopping trip.

I planned to see the doctor first thing in the morning.

The doctor gave me an electrocardiogram and said that everything looked normal. He asked me questions like, "was I worrying about anything? Was I having an unusual amount of stress? Was I harboring unexpressed feelings?"

WAS I EVER!

I never realized that all of that could wreak havoc on my mind and body. He diagnosed it as a full-fledged panic attack.

The doctor put me on a tranquilizer called Librium. They worked wonders for me, as I didn't give a rat's ass about anything. They put me in a relaxed, calm state.

I would sit on the porch for hours, just rocking in the chair, staring into space. It didn't keep me from doing my job or taking care of my daughter. It just took the edge off.

☆

Robbie had asked me on Friday if we could get together the next day. It would seem that his wife was going to a baby shower and he had a few hours to himself.

He picked me up at my house on Saturday afternoon and we spent a few hours at a motel, still with no intercourse. We fooled around and just enjoyed each other, took a shower together and headed home. It was just nice to be able to be together. It didn't happen enough.

Several weeks later, Tom called me again and asked if he could take me to dinner, he said he wanted to talk. I said, "Okay, just dinner and talking. That's it."

I should have known that would be a huge mistake. Why did he have this hold on me? I knew I was okay as long as I didn't see him. After dinner he parked the car on a street a few blocks from mine.

"Maybe we could see each other again," he said, "I know I wasn't a good boyfriend to you, and if you give me another chance, I'll show you I have changed."

He promised he would stop drinking and treat me better. "I missed you so much and I love you!"

I told him not to call me. I wanted time to think and get things together in my head.

I took a month off from Tom and Robbie.

The next month I agreed to go out with Tom a few times with no sex or kissing. He had a lot to prove to me and he had a lot to make up to me.

If he was still drinking, I didn't see it. He was on time for every date. He was trying hard and unbeknownst to sweet Robbie, I was seeing Tom again. And again, that guilty feeling was raining down on me once more. Only now the tables were turned and Robbie was on the hurtful, receiving end.

At the end of a date with Tom, we parked outside of my parent's house. Sitting there in the car, Tom took out my ring and begged me to take it back and put it on.

"Listen," I said, "if I take it back, no more dragging your ass on getting married! I'm not waiting forever, I have a child and I want to be married!"

He agreed to my terms so I put the ring back on.

Now I had to go through the task of telling Robbie and that was going to be the hardest thing I thought I would ever have to do. Way harder than when I broke it off with Tom because he deserved it. Robbie didn't deserve this. He was nothing but sweet to me and always treated me like a porcelain doll.

I would lay in bed that night, unable to sleep. Was I doing the right thing? Perhaps not, but Robbie was never going to leave his wife and I didn't want to be someone's part-time lover for the rest of my life!

I was ready for marriage. I was anxious to cook and to clean and to take care of my husband and child. That was what I needed now and Robbie just couldn't give me that.

I still loved Robbie and I loved Tom too.

I didn't have to say anything to Robbie the next day at lunch. He spotted the ring on my finger as we were sitting on the loading dock behind the factory. I was sitting on his lap when he asked, "why do you have that ring back on?"

Sadly I said, "I went back with Tom over the weekend." I can still remember the hurt, crushed look on his face. He didn't know what to say so I just put my arms around his neck and held him tight. Tears welled up in my eyes and I sobbed, "I never wanted to hurt you." And as I pulled away I saw tears in his eyes too.

It was heartbreaking and a day I never wanted to relive. He promised, "if you ever need me, I'll be there." After that day, whenever we saw each other, we would just smile, talk and be friendly to one another.

It was October now as Tom and I started to plan our wedding. Tom being Irish, I set St. Paddy's Day for the date of the ceremony. I also tried to use the color green in the plans whenever I could.

Green is a tricky color. The right amount equals a tasteful and thoughtful Irish wedding. Use too much and it's a tacky, drunken affair.

Two of my friends from the factory were going to be my bridesmaids and I asked Mary to be my Maid of Honor. Deep down I wished it could have been Ellen.

We all took a trip to the bridal shop one Saturday afternoon. The girls were told to choose whatever they wanted as long as it was green. My two bridesmaids would be in a darker shade of emerald green and my Maid of Honor in a lighter, mint green color. They found their dresses and put down deposits.

We all went to a smaller shop down the street to see about my dress. The seamstress showed me a pretty dress that was antique white with eyelet lace trimming and a sweetheart neckline. I asked if the white satin ribbon could be changed to emerald green velvet. She told me she would make it however I wanted.

My grandfather was a member of The Young Italian, Young Americans Club, or "The Yik-Yak," as everyone called it. Because he was a member, he was able to reserve the clubhouse hall for half of what it would cost a non-member.

The wedding was set for March 17, 1976. I took it as a lucky sign for us that St. Paddy's Day fell on a Saturday that year.

Over Thanksgiving weekend, I looked over apartment listings in our local newspaper. I found an apartment for rent that was only four blocks away from my parent's house and six blocks from Kim's school. It fell within our budget too.

I called the realtor and he said he could show us the apartment on Thanksgiving night. I called Tom right away and told him we had plans to see it after we finished with dinner.

The apartment was perfect for us, so we signed the lease and put down our deposit.

While Tom and I were broken up, his parents threw him out of the house. He moved in with Vince, who was a childhood friend of his.

Vince was a chubby, slightly balding guy who wore glasses. Basically, he was a loser, with no goals, dreams or future. He could be labeled a loser with the ladies too.

I didn't care much for him but I tolerated him for

Tom's sake.

Tom told me that after we married, he'd like me to quit work so I could spend more time with Kim but I knew the real reason. He didn't trust me, and this was his way of keeping me away from Robbie.

I agreed because I thought the temptation might be a little too much for me too. It would be a nice change for me.

The girls at work gave me a bridal shower. My in-laws also threw me a shower. Between both parties, I pretty much got everything I needed.

I was getting excited about the apartment, I picked up curtains for the windows, a bucket full of cleaning products and planned to take the next day off from work to clean the apartment and hang the curtains.

I opened the door to find cheap carpets on the floor, some dirty dishes in the sink, and a bed in both bedrooms. I was furious! Who in the hell was living in our apartment? It wasn't until I saw the girly magazine on the floor that I figured out that it was Vince.

I took out my lipstick from my bag, and wrote on the mirror, "Call me the minute you get home!"

Tom called right away and came over to my parent's house to explain. He told me that he and Vince had gotten thrown out of their apartment, so since we were not getting married until March, they were going to stay there.

I was mad and got right in Tom's face, "I don't care if you're staying there but I want him out and you tell him we're getting married sooner and I am moving in!"

I had toasted all of my wedding plans. I cut off my nose to spite my face. I didn't care.

I changed the date to December 31st and we

would get married by a Justice of the Peace on New Year's Eve.

I told Mary and my bridesmaids at work the next day. The first thing everyone asked was if I was pregnant. I assured them I was not. I felt bad because the store would not refund their money. I took a loss on my deposits too.

I called a few weeks before Christmas to arrange my wedding downtown and was told there were no slots open. Next, I called Yerky's which was a popular wedding chapel with no luck there.

I called the Justice of the Peace in the next county. I was trying everything to get this show on the road but the earliest date I could get was January 17th.

I was just thankful no one was mad at me. Getting married by a Justice meant I could only have one person there and it had to be Mary. My other two bridesmaids understood and of course would be at my wedding reception that my in-laws were planning to throw in their basement.

I had a dress in mind, but finding it would be the trick.

Two weeks before the wedding, I took the elevated subway into downtown. I went into every store and I couldn't find the dress I imagined or anything that remotely resembled it.

I was looking for an ivory satin dress with short sleeves and a pendulum waist. This dress shouldn't have been that hard to find, but I was wrong, it was. I came home exhausted and without a dress for my wedding.

I tried again in another shopping area with only days left. I was running out of time and I settled for a red and white dress. I hated it.

January 17th was here. I was to be married on one of the coldest days of the year without flowers or my parents.

There was no room in the car for them. There was only room for Tom, Mary, my future brother-in-law Paul, and my future father-in-law who was driving us.

After we were married, we came back to my in-law's house for that small reception they planned and the gifts we received there were mostly monetary.

It was pretty stupid of me to quit work because we really needed the money but Tom would rather rough it than have me anywhere around Robbie and because we didn't have much money, we planned to stay in a suburban roadside hotel for a week. This would be our honeymoon, just the two of us.

I even watched a football game with interest on Sunday with Tom and I hated football! I was having a good time, and I thought Tom was too until he called his father after dinner on Tuesday night. He hung up the phone and said he had to leave and stay with his father because he had a bad cold and wanted his son to take care of him.

"What?" I said, "you're going to cut our honeymoon short because your dad has a cold?"

It made no sense as his stepmother and both brothers still lived with his father and I wondered why they couldn't take care of him. I could see if he had a stroke or a heart attack but a cold? Really? Something just didn't smell right to me.

I said, "Fine. Take me to my parent's house. I'm not spending my first night in that apartment alone."

He spent four nights at his father's. When I called and asked how he was and he would tell me that he was doing better. I said, "Okay, that's it. You'll meet me at the apartment now, it's time to come home." And he did.

Kim had to stay at my parent's house for a few weeks without me because we didn't have a way of getting her new bed over to the apartment. We had to wait until a friend of Tom's got his truck fixed.

I decided to check all of the cards we got from the wedding because we were running out of money. When I did, I found that they were all empty. It would seem that Tom beat me to it.

"Where is the money from the cards?" I asked.

He looked at me like I was stupid and said, "how do you think I paid for the hotel?"

Tom and I stayed at our apartment with nothing but a mattress on the floor. We had no money.

Tom's uncle called and asked if we could use a kitchen table with chairs and we said "yes." We had to decide what to get first when we got our tax returns. We agreed on a bedroom set. Tom's father ended up helping us get our living room set. Tom's sister Barbara gave us a small TV and Tom's other sister gave us tables for the living room, a coffee table, and two side tables. With the money from Tom's first paycheck as a married man, I purchased two lamps.

It wasn't long after we were settled in, and with the comfort of that, Tom started drinking again and staying out late.

Friday night habits from when we were dating returned and he would stay out all night drinking his hard earned money.

Only once did I go to the bar to drag him home. I walked three blocks with Kim in tow. It was raining and I was getting angrier with every step I took. I threw the door of Curran's Bar open. It made a huge bang noise and I thought I might have broken the glass. I didn't, but I didn't give a shit if I did.

Every man in there each looked at the door expecting to see their own "old lady" and were quickly relieved to see it was some other poor sap's "old lady".

I didn't use the "Women's Entrance" that was on the side of the building, I walked through the front door and scanned the room for Tom's face but he wasn't there.

I thought about what I would have done if he was there and I didn't like what I was thinking.

I turned around and walked out of the bar without saying a word. Something tells me this was an everyday occurrence at those corner bars.

Before I moved in, Tom became friendly with the young couple upstairs. They hadn't been married for long either, maybe, only a few months.

As we came through the front door that first night Tom and I spent at the apartment, the door on the third floor popped open and out sprang two heads.

"We've been waiting for you all week!"

Her name was Denise and she was a cute girl with black hair. She and I immediately became really good friends.

Her husband Pete was a tall guy with sandy colored hair. He was handsome. Denise and I would do everything together. We went to the laundromat up on the avenue, food shopping, and spent the days together hanging out while the guys were at work. We'd often make dinner together and the four of us would eat at their apartment.

I would walk Kim to school every morning and then stop and have coffee with my mom. Sometimes Mom and I would go shopping or just spend the day together. I missed my parents and marriage was hard for me to get used to.

I didn't exactly have the model husband, but I never felt sorry for myself. After all, I made my bed now I had to lie in it.

Life with Tom wasn't all bad. When he was sober, he was funny and always made us laugh. When times were bad, I would think about Robbie and sometimes, I would cry.

I would miss him so badly and other times I would look at my pictures that I left at my parent's house. Pictures of Alex and Ellen and how those great times at the shore were the best times of my life.

Tom and I would fight a lot. The fights were mostly about his drinking, the staying out all night, about money, and about his parents. It would seem if we had plans, all it took was a call from his father or his stepmother and our plans were nixed.

It just seemed that I was never first in Tom's life. There was always someone or something taking preference over me.

To avoid fights, when he went out I would pack up Kim and spend the night at my parent's house. I had hoped that if he spent a few nights alone maybe he would get it.

He never did get it. He would just come home and pass out in bed but always managed to get himself to work the next day.

The guys would cover for him while he slept it off in the back of a bus while it was parked in the terminal for maintenance. This went on for a year.

During this time, Denise became pregnant so she and Pete decided to look for a house. They found one pretty fast and it wasn't that far from us but I didn't drive and would have to take two buses to see her.

I was devastated. We had become good friends and I was going to miss her very much.

The day came when they packed up to move. Denise and I stood outside of the apartment building hugging each other and crying. Our husbands had to pull us apart.

When that truck pulled away it was like losing Ellen all over again. It was at that moment that I made myself a promise. I would never get tight with another friend that way again. For days after, I was depressed and could do nothing but mope around. I had no one to pal around with. I felt alone and abandoned.

A few weeks later a girl from England took the apartment upstairs with her daughter. We became friendly but it wasn't the same, not like it was with Denise.

It was almost two years later, while taking a walk to a new supermarket that opened at Keystone and Robbins Streets, I discovered a new apartment building under construction. It was just a few blocks from where we lived.

The sign outside read "Available In Weeks," and there was a phone number. I called to get more information so I could tell Tom when he got home. I thought maybe we could start over in a new place.

The realtor called a few days later. We went right down to look at the model apartment. The owner met us out front. The apartment we would take had a private entrance up a set of stairs on the side of the building.

Once inside, there were five steps leading up to the living room. The living room flowed right into the opened dining area and through a threshold was a small kitchen. Down the middle of the hallway was one bathroom, across the hall from that was a utility room with a washer and dryer and two bedrooms were at the end of the hall.

I loved it because everything was brand new and had a clean, freshly painted, new carpet smell.

Tom and I agreed that we could take it and we made a fast Sunday morning move. It was a quiet little neighborhood.

Kim was only two blocks from her old friends and began making new friends on the street quickly.

I kept my promise to myself and would just say hello to my new neighbors. I would not let myself get close with anyone there.

Tom, always following in his father's footsteps, wanted to become a cop.

His father, once again, pulled some strings and arranged for Tom to take the test. He was hired by the local port authority as a patrolman but would now need to go to the police academy. He worked hard and graduated.

I thought, maybe now, he would be happy and grow up a bit. I hoped his drinking days would be over.

Things only got worse. Tom just wasn't a family man and he was never going to be. I would just learn to live with that.

There were mornings I would wake and Tom wouldn't be in bed all night, and I would look out our front window to see Tom sleeping it off in the car of our driveway. I would be the one embarrassed, not him.

Some of the bills were not getting paid, and the rent was always late. The phone would be shut off or the lights would go out and I knew that Tom took the money for drinks instead of paying the bills.

Tom expressed to me that he needed my help. I would have to go back to work because he couldn't pay for everything with just his pay. I said, "maybe if you paid the bills first and stopped spending half the money on drinks we would be alright." His answer to that was, "you wanted to move here, so you have to help."

I thought it might not be a bad idea. Kim was in grade school now from 9 AM to 3 PM and there was no reason that I couldn't work so I checked the paper for want ads.

I read that Franklin's, a new casual dining restaurant, was opening. I went for an interview and got the job because of my restaurant experience. I was told to report the following Monday for orientation.

That first day, we were broken down into groups for the jobs we would be doing. I was the only female out of the ten cooks hired.

We all became fast friends going through the six weeks of training together. I learned everything there was to know about that kitchen. I was the only cook that knew how to flip eggs in a pan, so I had to teach the other nine guys how to do it.

The restaurant had the grand opening and right out of the gate, Sundays were our busiest day. We would have a line out the door all day long. That was when I was put on the line making eggs. I was quick. Whoever was making the eggs had to be quick as it was fast and furious work but the time went by fast. I was having fun.

In one year I became kitchen manager. That could have meant making my job was less labor intensive, but I wasn't like that, I believed in doing my share and I worked right along side the guys. I did no more or no less than anyone else.

I was also making friends with the servers, hostesses and dishwashers. We had a close knit family that even included our bosses. We celebrated each other's birthdays, weddings, and at parties, we would all go together. We would even go out to dance clubs.

I became good friends with a waitress named Terry because she and I would have to open the restaurant at 5:30 AM. She would pick me up and drive me home every day.

Even though I was working, our financial situation

didn't improve. Tom was still getting drunk and spending money we didn't have and I tried to stash a little away so if something came up, I would have money.

I bought a lock box and hid it in my closet. So many times I had to use that money to make up the rent.

One day I came home from work to find that the lock box was broken into. All of the money I saved was gone and Tom didn't come home all night.

That was it. I couldn't take any more, so when Kim came home from school, we both packed up what we needed and went to my parent's house. I thought again, "maybe he will wise up when we don't come home. He'll see how much he needs us."

Tom called my parent's house the next day and asked what I was doing over there?

I told him as long as he's stealing money, that would be it for us. I threatened to stay at my parent's and I told him I didn't know if we were coming back to him.

After four weeks of separation, Tom called and said, "I want to talk to you." I knew that it would be the same old song and dance…"I'm sorry and I won't do it again."

I, like a fool, fell for it again. I didn't know what this hold was that Tom had on me. Like a fool, I went back home the next morning. I walked in to find a sink full of dirty dishes, glasses with mold growing on them and a hamper full of dirty clothes. The bed sheets weren't changed since I left.

I would ask myself again, "what was this hold that he had on me? Why am I here?"

It took me three days to get the apartment back the way it was, and I vowed never to do that again. The next time I leave it would be for good.

Tom's good behavior lasted for only one week and we were right back where we left off.

I had to tell myself not all of my time was bad with Tom. I'd brainwash myself into believing that we had good times now and then.

Tom did help me achieve some goals. He was a giving man. If someone liked his shirt, he would take it off and give it to him or her. If he could only stay sober, how much better life would have been for him and his family.

As a sober man, he was hilarious. Kim and I would laugh a lot. "Drunk Tom" was a monster.

I spent most of my time alone. I was getting used to it. If he didn't go out I would question him on why he wasn't.

Three years of living in that apartment was enough. The neighborhood was changing, the pig downstairs was arrested for child molestation, the roof was leaking, and mold was growing behind the wall.

I came home one day to find Kim's bedroom ceiling bulging in the middle. It was full of water and in front of my eyes, the bulge turned into a waterfall.

The landlord became a slumlord. The last straw was when I turned on the dining room chandelier and short-circuited the whole apartment. Seemed water accumulated from inside the ceiling through the wiring and into the chandelier and all of the bulbs exploded.

We used the poor maintenance issues as an excuse to not pay our rent, but that didn't mean we had saved any of the rent money.

I started looking for another place for us to live because we were so behind on our rent we would never be able to dig our way out of that hole even if they came in and made all of the repairs.

Besides all of that, I didn't feel safe staying there alone at night when Tom had to work the nightshift.

I began looking in the paper and saw a house for rent in the next neighborhood over. It was sixty dollars a month more than we were paying for that apartment, and we would be getting a whole three bedroom house.

Tom and I went to look at the house and we took it. This was our chance to start fresh!

Once again we made the early morning move, sneaking out while owing the landlord several months back rent.

Tom was climbing the ladder at work. He was getting promotion after promotion, thanks to his father of course. He was now a Commissioner. With that position, he had to attend meetings and that meant a lot of drinking. In that time he managed to crash and total three cars. The last accident he had it was a wonder he'd made it out alive.

He was also seeing other women.

☆

One night I awoke to hear him talking to someone on the phone downstairs. I picked up the receiver in the bedroom and heard him telling some woman, how much he adored her and wanted to be with her. She asked him "what about your wife?" and his answer was, "she doesn't understand me."

I came down the stairs, and said, "who are you talking to?"

He looked at me brazenly and said to her, "Speak of the devil, she's right here. I should hang up now." then passed out on the couch from intoxication.

There were the late night calls from other women. So you could add "unfaithful" to his resume also.

I began to seek attention from other men. There was a casino bus driver who would come into the restaurant and asked if I would make him special ordered "home fries". We made our breakfast potatoes a different way than he wanted so when I made them his way, he returned the next day with one long-stemmed rose. When he saw me waiting for a bus, he would pick me up in the casino bus and drive me home.

I would also flirt with the guy that delivered bacon and sausage to the restaurant. I would pour him a cup of coffee and he would sit and talk to me on my break. All I had to do was give him the okay, and I could have had him.

I ran to the convenience store a few blocks from

our house one day and when I was going in, Robbie was coming out. I was surprised and happy to see him. It had been almost ten years since I'd last seen him.

"What are you doing around here?" I asked him.

He said he was coming from his credit union that was on the corner. He told me I looked great and I told him he didn't look too bad himself.

He asked if I was still married to that guy.

Why did I have to say "yes?"

He asked if I was working and I told him the name of the restaurant and where it was. I invited him to stop in one morning and offered to make him breakfast. He said, "maybe I will."

I had forgotten how handsome he was, and even though I still thought about him, I didn't have any pictures of him like I did Alex. Sometimes your memories get foggy and faces blur and distort.

I wondered if he would come for breakfast or if he'd just said "maybe" to be polite.

The first week after that meeting, I would keep a watchful eye to the door. I'd watched the parking lot for cars that looked like his.

After a few weeks I started to give up hope until one morning I looked up one day to see him standing there smiling at me. "Can you take a break?"

I had my apron off like it was on fire and we sat at a table in the back of the dining room. The back table was behind a wall and only used when the restaurant was full. It was not considered the best seat in the house but it was more secluded. I felt the need to hide back there, as Tom would stop in from time to time.

We sat and made small talk. He told me he had two children now, a boy and a girl, and showed me their pictures. They were as gorgeous as their daddy I told him, and he just smiled.

I could always see a little twinkle in his eye that said he really did care for me. I was happy to see it was still there. His eyes always spoke to me. He was not like Alex, where I never really knew where I stood.

After that day, Robbie would come in whenever, when he could. We would sit and flirt with one another, but we never crossed the line. We never touched, because I never gave him the "go ahead," but there was something between us that never went away.

Late one night Tom came home drunk, and tried to force himself on me. I hated sex with Tom when he was drunk. He would take forever to finish and then there were times he would just pass out while in the act.

To avoid that mess I refused his advances. He became furious and as I was trying to fight him off, he grabbed my finger and pulled it back. I heard a loud crack and then what felt like a lighting bolt of pain. I screamed out and after a few more seconds of struggling, he gave up and went to bed.

I crawled into bed along side my daughter, shaking and sobbing until I fell asleep.

The next morning I went to work, making up some story to Terry that I banged my hand on the door jamb. As the day went on, my finger started to swell. I wore a gold and jade ring that Tom had given me on that finger. I should have taken it off while I was still able, but I didn't. By the end of my shift, my finger was swollen to the size of a breakfast sausage and the ring was cutting off my circulation.

I called Tom and said, "this is your fault. Come get me and take me to the hospital."

After they cut off my ring, they took x-rays and

told me my finger was broken. I had to wear a splint on it for five weeks. I never missed a day of work and Tom never even said he was sorry. I know he felt bad but still said nothing.

Weeks later, we had just gotten done eating dinner at my parent's house when my mother came into the living room saying "look what I found today." She unrolled the poster sized picture of me and Alex captured in that perfect moment.

Tom jumped up and snatched it from my mother's hands. "Let me see that!" he said, as he took one look and ripped it in four pieces then threw them on the table.

My heart wrenched, like he just ripped my heart from my chest, tore it into four pieces and tossed it on the table. It was my cherished picture of Alex but I acted like it didn't faze me.

"Is that supposed to bother me?" I said, holding everything inside. I slowly and coolly picked up the pieces, walked to the trash can and discarded it.

It was time to go home and he went out first to start the car. I ran into the kitchen retrieved my destroyed picture from the trash and put it in my bag.

When we got home I put it in a good hiding place and the next day I taped it together.

Ripping that poster gave Tom satisfaction but how would he feel if he knew he could never rip Alex from my heart. EVER!

When I talked to my mother the next day I had to ask why she would show that picture in front of Tom like that? She said she didn't think he would rip it up even though she knew Tom was always jealous of Alex.

I had taken care of that picture all those years and

now it was in pieces. I hated Tom that night because that was something sacred to me.

My mind started to wander back to that amazing time in my life. I wondered how Alex was now and if he'd ever married? Was he still as handsome? I was almost sure he was. Just to think about him made my heart feel warm. That was my satisfaction, knowing that he could still do that to me after all these years.

Life continued down the same path. Tom was still drinking, we still fought over bills and money, and I was still working at the restaurant.

Most of the guys who opened the restaurant with me had moved on to other restaurants so now there were only two cooks working a shift. The work was demanding but I stuck with it. I had seniority built up and I got most of my demands met. If I wanted a raise or requested special day off, I would get it. Best perk of all? I was still getting the occasional visit from Robbie.

I was making a stop at our neighborhood supermarket after work one day to pick up dinner. As I walked in, I saw a bulletin board. Mostly it was posts on 3x5 cards advertising rooms for rent or missing pet pictures, sale announcements and things of that nature. Out of the corner of my eye, I caught a glimpse of a flyer. It was for a fundraiser and as I read on, it said "Hosted by Alex Bentley."

I went weak in the knees just reading his name.

My adrenaline was pumping frantically and I could hardly control my excitement.

I copied the phone number down and briskly walked home. I'd left the store without food! I couldn't think about dinner at that moment. I was consumed with getting the tickets so I could see Alex again. I swung open the door, threw my keys and ran directly to the phone to call Terry. I didn't even take my jacket off. I asked her if she would go with me and she said "yes." The two of us could easily get the other girls from work to go, making it a night out with co-workers.

After explaining my story to all of my friends they were more than happy to be in on it. I rushed over to pick up the tickets after work the next day.

I had three weeks before the event and I could not think of much else. Every night after dinner, Kim would go to her friend's house to do homework and Tom would go out and do whatever it was that Tom did.

I would be alone with my fantasies. I'd put on my favorite music, lay on the couch, and dream of how the night was going to be. When Alex and I would be together again.

The next day at work, Terry's friend came in for breakfast.

She shamelessly flirted with him whenever she could.

Terry was a chubby girl with short brown hair, and a wide smile. She had been married several years and had two sons, but that wasn't going to stop her from getting what she wanted. She wanted Hank, a plumber that came in almost daily because he liked Terry too.

Terry invited Hank to the fundraiser. She was to

meet him in the parking lot and this was to be their first time alone together.

She would often joke how she would "jump his bones" if she ever got the chance.

The day finally arrived and Terry was scheduled to pick me up at 7 o'clock. Kim was spending the night at my parent's house. Tom dropped her off and then he did whatever. I couldn't give a rat's ass. This night was all about me and to say I didn't need a night about me was just plain wrong.

After a soothing hot bath, I started to get ready. I had to look good tonight, as it was the first time seeing Alex since that amazing night we spent together down the shore.

My hair was still blonde, extremely blonde, and now shoulder length. I don't recall how I wore it that night, but it was the early 80's. I probably curled it with my giant barrel curling iron. We'd all wanted hair like Farrah Fawcett.

I wore blue denim jeans and a pink satin blouse and moccasins. I had a bad case of butterflies in my stomach. What will I say to him? How will I approach him?

It seemed like an eternity waiting for Terry but she picked me up right on time.

We were meeting the other girls out front because I was holding everyone's ticket.

Walking through the doors, I could hear the music playing loudly. With each step I took, the sound of the music was being replaced by the beating of my own heart.

My legs were barely carrying me. As I turned my glance to the stage, Alex was sorting records, just like he was doing the first time I saw him fourteen years ago and he was just as handsome as ever. He hadn't changed a bit! I only hoped that I hadn't changed to him.

Terry nudged me to go over and say hello.

"I can't. Not yet. I have to sit and get my nerve first."

I tried to acting as nonchalant as I could around my girlfriends, but truth be told, I was as giddy as a schoolgirl.

Terry looked at her watch and said, "well, I hate to leave you alone, but there's a backseat with my name on it." I watched Terry make a beeline for the parking lot so I approached the stage and called out to him over the loud music "Alex!"

He looked down at me and I asked, "do you remember me? It's Sarah, from the Moonbeam Ballroom?"

His smile suddenly stretched from ear to ear. He bent down and said, "sure, I remember you. How could I ever forget those cute little dimples?"

I asked how he had been and he answered, "I'm good. And how about you? What have you been up to?"

"Mostly work," I said.

He asked if I had any request, "can I play something for you?" and an instant it came to me "oh sure, play "Bahama Mama" for me."

He turned and asked his assistant to put it on next and we continued to talk. He asked if I was married and I said yes, and that I had one daughter. I asked about him, if he married and he said "no, not me."

The assistant came back over to tell Alex that he didn't have my request. Alex said to me, "I think I left it home, would you like to take a ride with me to my house to get it?"

The words were no sooner off his lips, when suddenly a vision flashed across my mind of Alex and I stopping at a red light. In the next lane, my husband Tom leering at me! I wouldn't know how to even begin explaining that one!

Another fork in the road and again, I chose to say no. I told him that it was alright, that he didn't have to leave to get the record. Right after I declined I could feel that decision biting me right in the ass.

Another opportunity turned down and how I continued to let Alex's advances fall on deaf ears. I danced a little while longer while the decision danced around my mind.

When I got back to the table, Terry, now grinning from ear to ear, asked how it went. When I told her what he asked me, she said, "you're going, right?"

"Are you crazy? Are you nuts?" I laughed and said "I told him no!" Terry knew that my marriage was shaky and she would have given her blessing for me to go.

Maybe I should have gone, but knowing myself the way I did, the guilt of being unfaithful to Tom would have eaten me alive. I just couldn't do it. That, or it was the fear of getting caught with Alex. What was the worse that could have happened? Tom would egg Alex's house? Maybe, if it was 1975. But Tom was now a cop with a gun. Tom was a cop with a gun that got drunk.

The night came to a close and it was time to leave. I walked up to the stage to say goodbye to Alex.

"It was great seeing you again, Sarah." And I told him it was great seeing him too.

I had asked Terry to drop me off at my parent's

house because I didn't feel like dealing with Tom. My only want was to lie in bed and think about Alex.

I didn't think of too much else for weeks. I couldn't get Alex out of my mind. For me, it was like losing him all over again. I had my chance that night and I blew it.

Life is all about choices, and I made mine with the future in mind. There wasn't much I could do about it, I just had to be content with seeing him that night.

Not much changed in the months ahead. Tom was still drinking and Kim was starting high school. I was still working and going out with the girls once a month to blow off a little steam.

Work was getting hard now as we were down to one cook per shift. I opened in the morning alone, getting the food prepped for breakfast while cooking all of the orders. If that wasn't enough, I was also responsible for prepping the lunch shift and re-stocking the pantry.

And it didn't end there. If the guys from lunch shift were late, I would have to work until the next cook came in to relieve me. Might I add, the lunch cook was always late!

But wait! After the lunch cook would finally show, I would have to clean my breakfast station before being dismissed for the day.

To add insult to injury, every morning when I arrived, I would find the night shift did not do their cleaning or stocking duties.

I had many talks with my manager about this, but nothing was ever done so one morning I took pictures of the way I found the kitchen. I asked to see the district manager and showed him the pictures. After that meeting took place, things were a little better, but not by much.

During this time, my home life was getting worse as Tom's drinking was out of control. He was getting mentally and physically abusive and sometimes, I feared him. He would make a lot of threats. He would tell me "if you try to leave me I will kill you," "you'll never be able to get rid of me," "I will always be in your life," and the old "If I can't have you, no one can."

With four guns, and three of them being in the house I feared that one night he may get so drunk that I would experience one of them pointed in my face.

I was under so much stress that I began having anxiety attacks. Severe pain in my stomach and when they struck I had to succumb to the pain and lie down, even then it did not do much to relieve them.

I would put up with these attacks for a month. I went to see my doctor and he sent me for a number of tests.

A week had passed and I was called back to the doctor's office. He told me that I needed my gallbladder removed. I was frightened because I had never been hospitalized except to give birth.

I asked if it had to be done right away. He said that it wasn't an emergency, but he advised against putting it off any longer than six months.

Tom and I, along with Kim and my parents were planning a summer getaway to the Pocono Mountains.

We would go back to the same resort we vacationed at one summer earlier.

My mom and dad loved it. Dad would get up and sing at the nightly big band showcases. Anytime he wanted, they would give him the microphone and stage.

My Dad loved to sing. I believe this was a dream he had at one time. I just wanted to go and forget about the operation until vacation was over.

A month after we returned home, I couldn't stand the pain any longer so my doctor set up an appointment to talk with a surgeon.

He put my x-rays up on the light board. He studied them carefully, then turned to me and said, "who told you that you needed an operation?"

I told him my family doctor did.

"Well I don't see anything that indicates that you need your gallbladder removed," he continued, "this type of problem usually happens to women with the four F's."

I looked at him puzzled, "what does that mean?"

He held up his hand and counted on his fingers, "Forty, Fat, Fair and Fertile."

I heard, "Forty and Fat" and thought to myself, "the crust on this guy!" Just then, he redeemed himself by saying, "and you are only two of those, fair and fertile."

I really didn't know if he was pulling my leg with a straight face or not, but the news about not needing surgery was a relief!

He said, "go home and have your doctor look at these x-rays again. He's made a huge mistake as I am not seeing what he is seeing."

Robbie continued to make an appearance and stop

by whenever he could. It would always cheer me up and make my whole day more enjoyable.

A day or two before my birthday he came in work, and we took our hidden table in the back.

He said he came in to wish me a happy birthday!

"You remembered!"

"Sure I did. I'll always remember." Just like he'd promised.

After a short time chatting, I walked him to the front door, he turned and said, "I sure would like to give you a birthday kiss."

I grabbed him by his jacket and pulled him into the ladies' restroom. In there he took me in his big strong arms and delivered my kiss.

"Come on, we better get out of here before a woman walks in." I warned. He smiled and with that he was gone.

I knew Robbie still had feelings for me all I had to do was drop the checkered flag, and off to the races we would go, but I never did and he never pressured me either. Another choice made. Was it the right one? Maybe not, but for all I knew, Tom was still cheating on me. I would find matchbook covers with girl's names and phone numbers written on them, receipts from bed and breakfasts, bills for flowers from the florist and I knew I wasn't getting flowers.

What difference would it have made if I cheated on Tom? What's good for the goose, and all that? Right?

But that just wasn't me, I valued "marriage," but I guess I was married to Tom. Tom wasn't married to me.

He asked me to marry him but I forced him to marry me and I lived with that choice, no matter how wrong of a choice it turned out to be.

About a year later, I asked Tom to drive me to Woolworth's to pick up some things for the house. While walking through the aisle I spotted Alex! I started to approach him but I stopped dead in my tracks. He was mumbling erratically to himself.

If it were present day, I would have assumed he was on a cell phone with a Bluetooth device, deep in conversation, but it was 1986 and there were no small cell phones in the 80's.

He was talking to himself and looking around like he was lost. My first instinct was to help him but I was taken aback by his actions. It scared me a little and besides what if we began talking and he followed me outside the store? With Tom parked in front of the store, I would have witnessed the start of World War III for sure.

I stood back, watched him pay for his purchase and watched him leave.

When I left the store, I had seen that Alex was parked directly in front of our car. I don't think Tom was looking or noticed who it was.

As Alex pulled away, we were behind him at the red light. When the light changed, Alex made a right turn as we went straight.

I watched his car until it was no longer in sight and I worried if he was well. Why was he acting that way? It just didn't seem right to me and I prayed he was okay.

I was looking over the neighborhood paper one day, when I noticed an advertisement for another fundraiser. Alex was also hosting this one. It would be another chance to see him. I got on the phone to my girlfriends and once more they rallied to support me all the way.

For weeks, the anticipation sent me spinning into daydreams. Every chance I got, I thought of nothing but Alex. This time I was going to make it count!

My friends and I entered the fundraiser and found a table. Again the nerves were starting to kick in. I walked up to the stage but he was busy and didn't notice me.

He was still a handsome man. He didn't change much except his hair was a bit longer. I was glad he wasn't exhibiting the same behavior I saw the last time. In fact, he looked great and looked like himself again.

Just then he looked down, "Sarah, is that you?"

"Yes it's me. How have you been?"

He said he was well and asked if I wanted him to play "Bahama Mama." I told him I would love it.

He said he had been carrying it to every gig since he last saw me.

I asked him if he would dance a ladies' choice with me for old time sake. I asked him to play "Stay in My Corner" by The Dells. That was the one song that always made me think of him. It was number one that first summer down the shore.

He said "sure, if I can."

As I walked back to my table, I wondered what he meant by "if I can." It puzzled me but I dismissed it.

At last he had a ladies' choice and played my request. As soon as I heard the music start I headed for the stage. He was already jumping down to meet me on the dance floor and he took me in his arms.

He looked down and smiled at me. "I can't believe you have still got those cute dimples!"

"I suppose I will have them forever."

As we danced, he kept talking. I would have rathered he just danced and let me soak up what was happening at the time. I know my heart was beating out of my chest and I'm sure that he could feel it. I couldn't hide it.

> *There'll be times when I may fail*
> *I'll need your love to comfort me*
> *But if these may prevail*
>
> *But just a kiss from you*
> *Will make things sweet*
> *Mmm stay, oh stay*
> *One more time baby*
> *But just a kiss from you*
> *Will make things sweet*
>
> *Honey I love you,*
> *I love you,*
> *I love you*

I wanted to stay in his arms like that forever and wished the song would never end, but when it did he dipped me, and we both laughed and hugged.

The end of the night came quick. I walked to the stage and we said goodbye once again.

I always had regrets that I had not asked him out

for coffee afterwards. Any excuse to spend more time with him. I always looked for more fundraisers after that, but none ever included Alex.

Kim was starting to resemble Alex now.

She was tall in stature. Her smile and her interests were similar to Alex's. She even had his extroverted personality.

I held it close to my heart that Alex and I would have another chance to be together again. I didn't care how long it would take. I would wait forever if I had to. With that hope, I had the will to go on. Just knowing he was still on this Earth gave me a fighting chance.

He was my twin flame and whatever brought us together, whatever it was, I knew deep in my heart that we would be together again. If we were not together in this life, then we would surely be in another.

Tom was drinking even more now, if that were possible.

I remember a particularly bad week. There were union contract negotiations and Tom was arbitrator. He had to attend meetings all that week.

He would leave around 3 PM and not return home until the next morning, only to go to bed and get up and be out of the house again at three the next afternoon and not sober from the night before.

This went on for four consecutive days and nights. During this time, he totaled another one of our cars. It would seem he vomited while driving and lost control of the car and crashed into a storefront. Of course I didn't learn of this until a few hours later. He didn't come home. He had gone to my in-laws to sleep.

It was Easter Sunday and I got a call from him around 3 PM asking Kim and me to his parent's house for a big dinner.

I said "okay," and he said he would send his father's neighbor to pick us up. "Why can't you pick us up?" I asked. He said he would explain later.

My in-law's house was filled with friends, family and neighbors. My husband was busy getting sick in the bathroom as we all sat at the table eating.

When we got back home he told me the whole story. I shouted back at him, "how much more of this do I have to put up with? I can't take much more!"

I had made up my mind. I was leaving Tom. I couldn't deal with his bullshit anymore.

Unbeknownst to Tom, I went apartment hunting. I was planning on taking Kim and moving out. I couldn't find anything I could afford on my own and I didn't want to move in with my parents.

Tom said he wanted to talk, so one night after dinner he and I sat at the dining table.

Still mad as hell, I listened to him tell me that he was going to stop drinking. I can't tell you how many times I heard that one.

He continued to tell me that the week that just passed was a frightening one for him; he said he didn't remember driving home any of those nights. He was experiencing blackouts too.

He was visibly shaken up and promised this time he meant it. He was done. "I'm doing it for you," he said, "I know I have put you through a lot, and you stuck by me all these years. You're a good wife and you don't deserve this."

Of course I was leery of his hollow promises. I really had heard all of them so many times before, but I was willing to see what would happen.

After a while, I gave him the benefit of the doubt, but I couldn't help be nervous whenever Tom left the house.

Weeks of sobriety turned into months, months turned into years, and it would seem that Tom had indeed conquered his demons. At last, I was proud of him. He did it all on his own without help from a support group. Just fear and his own will power.

After that we never quarreled again. And as I had hoped, my stomach pains cleared up too. It had been my nerves the whole time aggravated by Tom's drinking and work.

The work at the restaurant was getting to be too heavy a load for someone now close to fifty. I would come home every night and bitch about my job and how unfairly I was being treated.

Tom was getting sick of hearing about it and snapped back one night, "why don't you just quit then? You come home every day complaining about it, and I can't stand to see you exhausted and burned out."

"I can't quit we need the money," was my response to which he came back with, "well it's not worth all of this; we'll get by just fine."

It didn't matter what Tom said, I wasn't going to quit without another job lined up.

There was a small delicatessen near my grandparent's house.

I stopped in one afternoon and asked them if they needed any help. It was a heavily Italian neighborhood.

Everyone there knew everyone else, and their grandchildren's children.

I was hired on the spot and would be working Friday, Saturday and Sunday mornings into the afternoons. That's when they were busiest.

I also accepted another job flipping burgers in a fast food restaurant on Monday, Tuesday and Wednesday. My work week was full and after the madness I'd just left, I could do both of these jobs with one hand tied behind my back.

I gave my notice and my last day at the restaurant was sad for me. Like I said, they were like family and I loved all of my coworkers, I just couldn't stand the job anymore.

They gave me a party complete with gifts and everyone signed a card for me. They told me that I would be missed.

I left instructions with Terry, that if Robbie ever came in again, to let him know I left the job.

That was the hardest part of quitting. I knew I would lose contact with Robbie, but if I stayed one more day on that job, I would have gone postal!

I never saw Robbie again and I had no way to get in touch with him. It never stopped me from thinking of him. I would just tell myself 'if it was meant to be, then fate will have us meet again."

But even more than Robbie, I missed Alex. I would sit on the edge of my bed whenever I was alone, look at my pictures and cry, missing Alex and my best friend Ellen.

I would have given anything to have them both back in my life again.

☆

It was a cold, windy late March afternoon, when Tom came home for dinner.

He had been at his parent's house and told me how it was strange, but his dad wrapped his arms around him and said, "I'm proud of you son. You have always been good to me and I want you to know that I love you."

His father was not affectionate to him before. This was what Tom always wanted to hear, for all of his life, and this must have been wonderful moment for Tom, except Tom wasn't as overjoyed as he should have been. Tom felt something wasn't right.

He said although his dad was getting ready for work, he didn't look well. My father-in-law worked as a night watchman at a warehouse.

The night went on like any other. After dinner, Tom went out. He was gone about two hours when I got a call from him telling me that his father suffered a stroke and was being taken to the hospital.

"Where are you?" I asked, "I'll be right there."

Tom just said "no, stay home. He is in a coma and I will be here all night. I'll call you and keep you informed."

This went on for days, I wanted to be there for Tom but he didn't want me there. I was hurt when I found out everyone was there but me. Was Tom trying to make me look bad by not having me there?

But that was only the tip of the iceberg. I worried

sick about Tom. Worried he may hit the sauce again being distressed like this. And what if his father died?

God forgive me, but I worried about myself.

I didn't want to see all of Tom's hard work to stay sober go up in smoke. Tom was so close to his dad, I had feared he wasn't going to be able to handle it, and again my life would fold like a house of cards.

I knew I couldn't go back the way it was.

Five days later, on a Saturday morning, Tom called and said his dad had passed on.

"Are you okay?" He answered with a solemn, "I'm fine. I am with my brother." He seemed okay when he returned home that afternoon.

A day or two later, Tom was in the bedroom, when I heard an ungodly wail. I ran upstairs to find Tom on the bed crying his eyes out. The reality of his father's death had just sunk in.

I tried to comfort him the best I could, but I knew Tom was going to have to mourn in his own way.

The day of the funeral, I felt like such an outsider. I was picked up by a friend of Tom's and taken to the church while the rest of the family members rode in limos.

The services had already started, so I took a seat in the back of the church. At the burial again I rode with Tom's friend, but once there, Tom did stand with me.

Even at the luncheon, I was put with a table of strangers and not with family. It wasn't until my sister-in-law, Barbara came over and told me to come sit at her table. I said there was no room for me but she said "we'll make room!"

Why was I being treated this way? I never forgave Tom for that day, I felt so hurt. I don't care how much he was grieving. He shouldn't have treated me like that!

As bad as it must have been for Tom, he never touched a drink, but the death of his dad changed him. He was always depressed, moody and sometimes just plain mean.

Intimacy with Tom was also different. As a way to let out his anger, he became rough, violent, and verbally abusive.

I would start to get bad headaches at just the thought of having sex with him. I did it to keep the peace, but got out of it as much as I could.

The following three years after his father's death, was one death after another in both of our families. Tom's youngest brother committed suicide first, then two of my aunts passed away a week apart, followed by my cousin and then my Godmother. A month after that Tom's oldest brother hung himself in jail and lastly, Tom's stepmother died.

Of course life can never be perfect but amidst all the death and sadness, money was not an issue. The bills got paid on time. Kim had moved to the city to work in fashion so with one less mouth to feed, I learned how to drive. I was a quick learner and in no time I had my license and Tom bought me my first car.

There would be times Tom would come in from work and be in a pretty good mood. In the time it would take for him to get out of his suit into his everyday clothes his mood would change to mean and angry. His behavior was bizarre.

Tom chose early retirement from his job as Commissioner. He said he would find something not so stressful. Jobs were not as easy to find as he thought, and one year turned into two and bills were piling up again.

He would lie and say he paid them. Tom liked to take money for his own enjoyment first, and important things he brushed off. His priorities sucked and he always thought he was one ticket from winning the lottery or something to pull his ass out of debt.

I needed to take a third job so I started to clean for a few older women whenever I could find the time. These women had friends that needed help too so I was able to give up the job at the Burger Hut. I wasn't making a lot of money, but it put food on the table.

Weeks later, the deli announced that the building was sold and they would be closing down. I let go of the wrong job.

It was alright though; I was getting older and couldn't work the hours. The work for the ladies wasn't too hard. Light dusting, some shopping, mostly being a friendly face they could count on seeing every day.

It pained me to think how these women had children of their own that would just leave them alone. Their kids would never call or visit, and if they needed help their kids would say, "have Sarah do it."

These ladies treated me like I was their daughter. They loved me, and all I did for them. It was rewarding.
They would give me gifts and on holidays I would make them a plate and deliver it to their houses.

Kim had met a nice guy and had moved in with him. She was happy and for that I was grateful.

I became interested in decorating and interior design. With my background in art and painting, I combined both passions and was able to get some design jobs.

My ladies I cleaned house for would tell all of

their neighbors. It was bringing in extra money, plus I was doing something I loved.

I decided to do something else for myself. I took a correspondence course for ten months to become certified as an interior decorator. I paid for my education on a monthly basis. I passed with flying colors! I received my diploma and certification and I was proud of myself!

I focused on decorative painting, recovering dining room and kitchen chairs, refinishing furniture and window treatments. I also went room to room in our rented house, redoing every room until they were all completely different.

My home was my showcase. I even constructed a faux fireplace for the living room. I made it out of plywood and I painted it trompe l'oeil to look like stone.

I always wanted a fireplace. I would put candles or wood logs in the opening until Kim gave me a prop lighting effect that she would use in window displays.

The fan would blow a piece of silk to look like fire and the light would shine up on the fabric so that it flickered.

It looked so real my landlord thought I was going to set the house on fire until I showed him that it was just a light.

☆

Hurricane Katrina had just devastated the Southern part of the U.S. Tom was still not working a steady job. One of Tom's friends heard of an opportunity to go and help rebuild. He asked Tom if he was interested as the money was good.

Tom came home and asked if I had a problem with him living in Louisiana for six weeks to help in the relief efforts.

I didn't have a problem with him going and I kind of welcomed the idea. I was looking forward to time alone.

I had my plans set before he even left. On the weekends I would redecorate the bathroom. It was perfect, as I would have no one under foot.

The wallpaper needed scraping off before I could paint. I wanted to paint a striped effect with gold glaze. Why I decided to do this in the middle of August with no air conditioning upstairs is a mystery, but it would keep me busy and I would be finished with the entire project by the time Tom returned home.

He left on a Thursday evening and called me every night without fail.

After six weeks, Kim picked me up and we headed for the airport to retrieve Tom.

When he spotted me, he smiled, and we hugged one another. I think he truly missed me, possibly more than I missed him.

I told him to go see what I had been up to while he was away. The first words out of his mouth were "WOW! It looks great, you're amazing!" What he loved most of all was the pull out shaving mirror I'd installed.

One thing I learned in my course was a good designer's job is to make everything functional, and although I did install it for him to use, my main reason was because he would open the medicine cabinet to shave and never closed it when he finished. So it really was a win/win.

He told me later that the mirror was one of the best gifts I ever got him.

Tom was only home for a week when they called and asked if he would like to come back for another six weeks?

He asked me again if I would mind. I told him if he wanted to go back it was up to him.

He left again and in a short while, I began feeling something wasn't right. Everything was different than his last trip there. The first few nights there, he would call then after that, he would either call late or not at all.

When I would call him it would always go to voicemail.

After three days of this, he called and said he had been sick. He told me a doctor and her husband was taking good care of him. "oh they just love me!" he said.

I said, "that's good," but I was getting a gut feeling something still wasn't right. When he came home this time it wasn't like before. I don't think he missed me at all.

Two weeks had passed since he came home. He

told me that he was going to Washington, DC for a follow up from when he was sick.

"Why can't you see our doctor?" I asked. He said the husband and wife team wanted him to come and spend the weekend there to see how he was doing.

Tom left on Thursday afternoon and took a train to Washington.

I didn't hear from him for four days. He didn't answer his phone and I began to worry. Maybe he didn't get there at all! When he didn't return home after the weekend I called his phone again. It went straight to voicemail. I left a message that I was worried. I began crying, "please call me. I don't understand what's going on? Let me know your okay!"

Mid-week, I received a call from him telling me the tests found cancer and that he had to see another doctor. He didn't call because he didn't want to worry me.

"Well," I asked, "when are you coming home?" His answer was, "I don't know," and he promised to keep me informed.

It would be a year before I found out the truth.

He returned home after a week away, and nothing more was ever said about his trip or illness.

☆

Saturdays were the only day of the week Tom and I would spend together, and not all day, only Saturday nights.

I did my thing and Tom did his. We were rarely home at the same time. We would not watch TV together anymore. We didn't even have our meals together.

Saturdays were different. We would have breakfast together at the local diner, take a day trip somewhere in the suburbs, or go out to a nice dinner and then to a mall for some shopping before coming home.

One Saturday morning, instead of going for a drive after breakfast, we came home from the diner. Tom was reading the newspaper and I was folding laundry. Tom and I were talking and I don't recall the topic, but out of nowhere, Tom said to me that he wasn't going to be around much longer.

I asked him what he meant by that and he said, "I'm going to die soon, so you might as well get used to the idea." I told him to shut up and that he didn't know when he was going to die, nobody knows.

I thought he was just mimicking his father who would always say the same thing. "I'm not a well man, I won't be around for too much longer," and "I'm going to die soon."

I even joked and said sarcastically, "okay, Jack," because Jack was what we called his father.

"Okay," he said, "just remember what I said."

And with that I left the room to put the laundry away.

Tom bought a shirt the week prior and was going to return it for fit. When we reached the store, Tom went into the trunk of the car for the shirt only to find he had forgotten it.

He flew into such a rage about it. He was like a madman!

"So what," I said, "we can bring it back later. What's the big deal?"

And then he turned his anger towards me, "What's the big deal?" he screamed, "I wanted to return it tonight, that's the big deal!"

I just left him huff and puff until he simmered down.

This night we decided to go shopping first and pick up a pizza on the way home.

When we returned to the car after shopping, Tom started clutching his chest. We had only been driving five minutes and were close to the hospital.

"Are you alright?" I asked him.

"I have those pains in my chest again." He would get them occasionally for the last few years. They were nothing a glass of ginger ale wouldn't cure, but tonight he was pale, and perspiring heavily.

"We are going right past the hospital. Pull over and let me drive," I demanded. He came back with a quick, "NO! I'll be fine!"

"You're not fine! Pull over!" and with that he drove right past the hospital.

"Well that was dumb." I said, "we're right here."

He promised that he would be fine. He told me that when we reached the pizza place, he would go in to get the pie. He insisted on going in.

As I sat in the car, I observed him pacing back and forth until he came out. "Let me drive the rest of the way home, so you can relax", I offered but he wouldn't have any of it! He was a stubborn one INDEED!

When we got home I asked why he wouldn't lie down across the bed and rest. I told him the pizza would wait.

He said, "no, I'm hungry," and he ate four pieces with no problem. Only after he was done eating did he lie on the couch.

After an hour, he seemed fine. The rest of that Saturday night went like every other. We watch a little TV and then I went up to bed.

I was just starting to doze off, when I heard Tom come to the bedroom door and say, "I'm having the pains again and I'm going to the hospital."

I was in a bit of a sleep haze, but I managed to say, "wait, I'll drive you, or better yet, call 9-1..." and that fast, I heard our front door close and he was gone.

Why in Hell was he so stubborn? He would make me so angry sometimes! I laid in bed, staring up at the ceiling. I could hear police cars speeding up the avenue, a few blocks away.

I got an eerie feeling that something was wrong. Just then, Tom's shift robe, where he kept his nice clothes, made a loud cracking sound and I jumped.

It wasn't more than a minute later and the phone rang. I answered and the voice on the other end asked, "is this Mrs. Tom Macpherson?"

I said only, "yes" and the voice said, "your husband has just been in an accident and I need you to come to the scene, right away." I told whoever it was that I would be right there.

As I drove to the accident scene, my insides were shaking. It was a weird feeling, best described as "liquefaction."

I could see flashing lights from the police cars ahead of me as the ambulance was just pulling away. Our car was wrapped around a pole. I parked my car, ran to a police officer and asked if my husband was okay.

He said they were on their way to the hospital now and he instructed me to follow him closely in my car. He said, "we're not stopping for any lights or stop signs."

I followed him, but he was driving so fast. I had trouble keeping up. In hindsight, it's an irresponsible policy.

When we arrived at the hospital, I heard someone calling my name. It was Barbara and my niece, Sandra. We all went into the waiting room together. We were told to go into an office, and to wait, and that someone would be in shortly.

I looked at my sister-in-law and said, "this doesn't look good to me." I sat there with my insides trembling.

I tried calling Kim but her phone went right to voicemail. I left a message saying, "call me when you get this."

A doctor came into the room we were waiting in. He had the bedside manner of cold fish. He simply stated they did all they could, and that Tom had flatlined in the ambulance. He'd died of a massive heart attack.

I tried three more times to get my daughter on the phone and each time it went to voicemail. By the third time I was trying to compose myself but pleaded with her to call me back.

All I can remember was my sister-in-law, flying off her chair and carrying on like I've never seen before.

I stood frozen and immediately thought to myself, "what was I going to do?"

There was so much I didn't know like how to take care of the cars and all of the things Tom used to do. "What was I going to do?" kept echoing in my mind. I felt so lost and alone.

I went in where Tom was lying. He was cold and white with a sheet covering him up to his chest. I kissed him goodbye and told him I loved him.

Everyone came back to my house with me. We sat like zombies and made small talk. I knew they were making sure I was okay. It was now 3:30 AM.

When everyone left, I stood on the front steps watching as one by one, they pulled away in their cars. I sat down on the step and just looked at the sky.

I tried once more to get Kim on the phone, but she wasn't answering. She was probably sleeping and had her ringer off.

I knew that by morning, she would know something was wrong. She would see how many times I called and at what time I was making the calls.

I continued to sit out on the step, in the dark on my quiet street of row homes. Everyone was asleep and I realized I was a woman outside, alone, at 4 AM.

I went back into the house, where I sat in my chair, staring out through the panels of glass in my front door. The black sky of night turned into the light of day.

I still could not believe it. Even though I saw Tom with my own eyes, and kissed his cold face goodbye, I still expected him to come walking through the door any minute.

Suddenly, the phone ringing startled me. It was now 7 AM and when I answered, it was an administrator from the hospital asking me if I wanted to donate any of Tom's organs.

"WHAT?" I said, "What are you asking me?"

The voice on the other end said, "I know this seems cruel right now, but you see we only have a small window of time. If you say yes, so we would need your answer now."

They were talking as though Tom was an old car, no longer in use, and they needed the spare parts! My husband had only been dead a few hours. Where was the compassion?

She asked me again, "I apologize, but we need your answer now."

"Then my answer is no!" I cried, "I just can't. I know it is a selfish thing to do, but having you spring it on me like you did, well, it's all too fresh. I can't handle it." And I hung up the phone.

Every Sunday morning, I would usually pick my parents up and take them food shopping. I was up all night so I left the house early.

I wanted to drive back were Tom had the accident. I don't know why, I just did.

When my nephew parked my car the night before, he had to park two blocks from the house. I walked up the street, as I did so many times in my life but on this morning everything looked distorted. The wide street looked narrow. It was still and I remember feeling strange.

I drove to the accident scene and pulled over along the curb. I would stare at the pole that Tom hit in disbelief.

Enough. I got back in the car and drove on to my parent's house.

Dad answered the door, took one look at me and knew something was wrong. I think he thought I probably had a bad fight with Tom.

He said, "you're early today."

I told him I had not been to bed and that I was at the hospital for hours. I told him that Tom had a massive heart attack and was dead.

My father, walking to his chair, whipped his head around and asked, "what?"

I repeated, "he's dead!"

My mother just put her head in her hands and said "oh my God."

It was a shock and no one was ready for it.

I told them I would wait in the car until they finished their shopping. I just couldn't face anyone that day, so I sat in the car and cried. I took them home and cried some more. When I got home, I got in bed and cried myself to sleep.

The phone rang, startling me again. It was finally Kim.

She knew something was wrong because I had called too many times and late at night.

She asked right away, "is it Poppy?" She was referring to my dad; she had always called her grandfather "Poppy."

I said, "no, it's Daddy. He died last night of a heart attack."

"I thought for sure something happened to Poppy, wow, I wasn't thinking this at all." she said. "Mom, let me tie up some loose ends at work, and I will be up to stay with you."

When I hung up from Kim, I called Tom's best friend, Sam.

He was smart. He could help me sort out a lot of things. Sam had been Tom's friend for years. Tom helped Sam get on the police force.

Sam was like everyone else, in shock. He said he would be over when he was through with work.

Sam had kept his promise and came right over. We talked about a few concerns I had, about things I had not a clue about, and he would help me for the next three months.

I would also get a lot of help and support from my brother-in-law and Tom's nephew.

I was grateful for my daughter's company. She stayed with me until after the funeral.

Sam would come over often. We would sit and talk, or go to dinner now and then, any way I could think of to thank him for his help.

I began looking forward to his visits. Let me be clear, I never had romantic feelings for him. I would get the feeling that he would have liked to play on my vulnerability if I would have let him.

Seems there's a silent oath among cops and firemen that came to light after September 11, 2001. Many policemen who survived left their wives for their fallen brother's wives. I wouldn't have been surprised if Tom and Sam had also taken this oath to each other.

While going through Tom's belongings, I came

across a greeting card. I read it. It was from a woman he had met while he was in Louisiana.

> *I am sorry you decided to go back home,*
> *but I understand. I'll be here if you*
> *ever change your mind and want to*
> *come back to me.*
>
> *I will always love you.*

I can remember the day the envelope came in the mail. I had a feeling I knew what it was. I was going to read it and never give it to him but instead I wanted to see him squirm out of it.

I gave it to him and said, "open it. Who's it from?"

He squirmed alright, and said, "I don't know." He took all of the mail and went upstairs.

I knew there was something he was hiding. I knew and, I would find out that Sam knew. Sam knew all about this woman. I asked Sam to be honest with me and I showed him the card.

He told me that she was a doctor in Louisiana, and that Tom was having an affair with her. She was pressuring Tom to leave me, to be with her.

Tom was telling me the truth. There was a doctor that loved him so much he just made up the part about her having a husband. Sam also revealed that she was who he stayed with that week in Washington, DC.

The sadness was replaced with outrage. I was no longer mourning for Tom. All of my grief ended in an instant.

All at once, I felt empowered and strong. I thought of it as a gift. I had finally woken up and for the first time, I saw Tom for who he really was.

I was going to be just fine by myself. I would have no more man to worry about. I was taking care of both of us for so long, that I could take care of myself just fine!

I remembered the priest at the funeral saying, "you never know the true man until after his death." It was spoken directly at me and it would take a week after Tom's funeral for it to ring true. I now knew the true man. I felt that my whole marriage had been a farce and I allowed myself to finally believe that Tom was never faithful to me.

I was going to put all of that behind me now. That part of my life was over.

Within months, my health improved. My headaches were gone. I never felt better in my life. I was working and taking care of myself, all on my own.

For two wonderful years, I experienced what it was like to be completely independent. I didn't have to be home by any certain time. I could eat meals when I felt like it and sleep as late as I wanted. That was, until my father's health began to fail.

He'd had a stroke, and after that, he was in and out of the hospital. It made things hard on my mother so I told them it was time they sell the house and move in with me.

After the stroke, Dad needed a pacemaker. He swore he had a weak heart caused by a bout of Rheumatic Fever when he was ten years old. He was told afterward he would have a heart murmur.

He'd already had prostate cancer a few years prior and undergone radiation therapy for thirty-three weeks.

They moved in and we sold the house.

Just one year earlier, houses in their area were selling for over $100,000.00. That quick, the housing market crashed and the most we could get for the house was just about half of that.

They were all settled in. I installed a chair lift, repainted the back bedroom. I bought them all new bedding, recliner chairs, and a new TV.

I had a schedule again. I had to prepare meals, be home by a certain time, take them both to doctor appointments, and do the shopping and laundry. Having them there was somewhat of a comfort as Kim and I both worried about them living alone.

Dad was starting to do better. His strength was returning until when he fell and broke his arm. It swelled up and oozed blood from his pores. Back to the hospital he went.

One week after he got home, he had gotten up in the middle of the night without asking for assistance. I don't know where he thought he was going. Perhaps he was sleepwalking but he fell and broke his hip. He had replacement surgery but never walked again. He stayed in the hospital, and then was moved to a rehabilitation center where he was given huge doses of morphine for the pain. The drugs sent him spiraling into Dementia and he was never the same.

On my visits he would tell me that all the nurses would take him out to clubs every night. They would drink and dance all night and during the day, he worked as the landscaper on the hospital grounds.

I would just go along with him since it was the

only way to have a conversation.

It was heartbreaking for me. My dad had always been a attractive man and to see him diminish like this was sad.

Over the last ten years we bonded. He would always say that he appreciated that I was taking care of him and on the bad days he would always say he was sorry. I would tell him that it was my pleasure.

The doctors told me how it would be best for everyone if I put my dad in hospice care.

The final decision I had to make was if he would be put on a feeding tube. He wouldn't have wanted that. Kim told me that, my mother told me that. I refused further treatment for him. He would last for only four more days.

Even though I had the support of everyone who was important to me, I still had guilt. Did I do the right thing? It was a hard decision for me to make, but Dad was terminally ill and was never going to get better.

Dad was gone, but before he broke his hip I did give him his only birthday party on what would be his last birthday and the whole family showed up.

Dad had me promise to always take care of Mom after he was gone and I agreed.

I thought with Dad gone, Mom and I could get a bit closer. I imagined us going out shopping or to the diner for lunch. Maybe we would take trips to the casino, but instead, Mom never wanted to do anything.

She only wanted to sit in her chair.

I gave her time. I thought she might have been a bit depressed for a while, which was understandable. They had been married for 63 years, and their marriage was good.

I know she missed him. I did too.

Mom started getting anxiety whenever I had to leave the house. She would think thirty minutes was three hours and this made my time out of the house extremely stressful for me.

I was limited to the things I could do. This was hard for me. I had always been active and always made good use of time, but my days became wasted, sitting with Mom so she would be content.

Even if I were out of the room for too long, she would ask me what was I doing? She'd ask why it was taking me so long to do certain chores.

Mom liked to bicker with me and that would work on my nerves. My mom and I use to be close, and I missed that, but Mom had now turned into a crotchety old lady.

I hadn't thought it would be like this, giving up so much of my own life when I promised Dad, "I will take care of her as long as I need to, she is my Mom."

I would visit Tom's grave, on his birthday and holidays the first two years after his death, but was still holding in anger of the betrayal I felt and went to the grave less and less. I had admitted to myself, that I was a lot of things, but a hypocrite was not one of them! I never was and never will be.

But that's what I felt like whenever I went to the grave; I just could not do it any more. I felt I gave up so much of myself for Tom. Two chances to be with Alex, a relationship with Robbie that, I was sure, would have lasted a long time even if we only remained friends.

I had lost respect for Tom, and he never had it for me.

Kim and I would talk every day on the phone. I would vent my problems, and she would always talk me down from the ledge, and I would feel better.

She's a wonderful kid, and I would ask myself, "how did I get so lucky to have a kid like her?" We had always had a close relationship, and she never gave me any trouble growing up.

It's why there isn't too much written in my story about her. She was the least of my problems. She was my best friend and my daughter and I could count on her for anything, I only hoped I had been a good mother to her.

I would think of all of those times I'd yanked her from our home to get away from Tom, to spend the night at my parent's house.

Some nights, it was dark and cold as we made our walk, only to find when we got there that she'd forgotten her homework, or her gym clothes. But through it all we were close and the formula worked for us.

One night after my mother had gone to bed, I decided to look up Alex on the computer. A few pictures came up along with some videos of his old dance shows.

Just looking at them stirred up all the old feelings again.

I thought that maybe I could contact him and we could get together. Maybe we could meet for lunch, my treat. After all, I was free and single again. I could live my life anyway I saw fit. I was almost positive that he would not be married.

I had worked myself into an excited tizzy, thinking I would lose that five extra pounds that I have been trying to shed for the last month. I'd exercise and diet to get myself looking good, and then I'd contact him.

I knew he would meet with me. That is just the way he was. Who knows what could happen as a result of this?

Whether or not this was going to happen, I was making huge plans. I wonder what he looks like now? I knew he was still handsome, and even if not he was still Alex, and I loved him unconditionally.

Maybe he would not be attracted to me now, after all these many years had passed. Maybe I should leave it alone, let him remember me the way I was the last time we were together dancing.

Anyway he will always be the Alex I first met, the Alex in my picture of us together, that picture of us kissing a moment frozen in time forever.

The next evening, I returned to the computer to see if I could find anything else about Alex. I typed his name in Google and suddenly this page came up. It was a message board where people were leaving messages of condolence. Alex passed away just a few months earlier.

In shock, I just stared at the brightly lit computer

screen. Reading the words, over and over again, I could not believe what I was seeing.

I could feel the tears welling quickly in my eyes, and one blink would send them streaming down my face like Niagara Falls. I sat still. I could not believe what I was reading.

It said that he had been terminally ill for years before his death. He had been ill when I saw him last, that's why he said, "if I can" when I asked him to dance.

As I closed the computer a flood of emotions charged at me, like hundreds of people all pushing to get through a revolving door at the same time.

Disbelief, sadness, helplessness, despair, and anger that my hopes for any kind of reunion had just been shattered.

It felt as though someone had ripped out my heart, tore it in half, and then put only half back. I felt like half of my life was torn away from me. I no longer felt whole. It was then that I knew, that Alex was the love of my life, my one true love. I had never felt that way about any man before, not the way I loved him.

The very next day, taking my mother to her Optometrist office, sitting there just crying uncontrollably in a waiting room full of people, staring at me, I didn't care. To me, they were invisible.

And the day after that, walking on my treadmill, watching Oprah on TV with Barbra Streisand singing "The Way We Were," I cried my eyes out some more.

It wasn't fair for Alex to be ill all of those years. Of all people, he didn't deserve that! It just made me so angry! He was such a good guy, nice to everyone, happy, sweet and wonderful.

His death had taken me down faster than TNT in

an abandoned building, and for the first time in my life, I understood the words to songs about love that I'd heard many times. Now it was like hearing them for the first time. Now the words had meaning like never before.

I could not eat for four days, and took off those five pounds that I wanted so desperately to lose, and with all the emotions I was dealing with, along came guilt.

I wanted him to know how much I loved him, and how much he meant to me. I was sure he never knew how much and it weighed heavy on me.

I never told him, or acted like he was that important to me, like the time I left him to get back to the dance, what could have been more important than spending the night with him? I guess I just did not want to seem that eager and in playing it too cool, he didn't think he meant that much to me.

Why did I do those things? I would just beat myself up constantly.

I was so sorry for that now, but if I had to do it all over again, I still would not do it any differently.

I never wanted to come on strong either, I wanted it to happen slow and smooth, and make him think it would be all his idea. But now it's too late. He will never know.

I was grieving for Alex, and never going to be able to accept this. Then when it couldn't get any worse, I became plagued with depression.

I had never believed in depression. I always thought it was just a word made up by people who couldn't pick themselves back up and dust themselves off but I soon learned that I had been thinking wrong.

It was just like that black cloud that follows you

wherever you go, and stays with you every minute of the day and night, like that unwanted houseguest that doesn't know when to leave.

You hate it so much, but some how you nurture it, and it becomes your constant companion that you can depend on it being there for you, though this bad time.

Actually, at times I thought I was losing my mind. I was thinking if I could some how just get to the seashore, everything would still be there, nothing would be changed, it would be years ago, and then everything would be ok. I could have it all again.

To add salt to the wound, summer was coming, that's when it all started for me.

Some nights it would be just the way a warm breeze would blow in my window, or the way the sky would look on a hot summer night. A song or a smell would bring it all back, and it would hurt, physically hurt, like a railroad spike being driven through my chest.

PART FOUR
Save The Last Dance For Me

I purchased a pretty frame for my picture of Alex and me. I'd look at it everyday. I looked at it so much that I do not have to look at again; the image is burned into my brain. I can close my eyes and tell you every detail of that picture, without looking.

It's been five months since I learned of Alex's death, and I am not better, I am still grieving and depressed.

I have tried so many ways to help myself. One way was to repeat my favorite poem over and over to myself every day. The way an alcoholic recites sobriety sayings.

The poem was Splendor in the Grass by Henry Wadsworth Longfellow.

What though the radiance
which was once so bright
Be now for ever taken from my sight,
Though nothing can bring back the hour
Of splendour in the grass,
Of glory in the flower,
We will grieve not, rather find
Strength in what remains behind;
In the primal sympathy
Which having been must ever be;
In the soothing thoughts that spring
Out of human suffering;
In the faith that looks through death,

In years that bring the philosophic mind.

The radiance, being Alex and the way he was, was now taken from my sight, never to see him again.

The splendor in the grass, the time that we had and now the past, and I should not grieve, but pull strength from what we had.

Beautiful words but hard to live by when your life feels so empty. It was like looking down a long dark hallway, with nothing at the end.

I began keeping a journal of my feelings everyday with the hopes that it would help. It became my therapy. I was hating the way I felt and was desperately trying anything that would help.

I began to write another book of poems, they were dark and gloomy. They were mushy about love and loss, because that's where I was.

I did write one poem that I became proud of. I think it captured Alex's spirit and our relationship.

The Butterfly

He flew from flower to flower,
As I watched him patiently
And prayed that I would have my turn.
Some day he will pick me.

It was just short of a fantasy.
Never thinking it would come true.
That I would spend such special times
Those times I spent with you.

Just to think of you every morning
Thrilled me to the core.
The times we were together
I just couldn't ask for more.

But like a free spirited butterfly,
Never landing for too long,
I watched you fly right through my hands
And suddenly you were gone.

Maybe belonging to no one
Was the way you had to be,
But I wished the dwelling flower
Could have turned out to be me.

This poem was helping me cope with my loss. But the truth of the matter was, I didn't just lose Alex, I lost him forty-three years ago. That did not lessen the pain. His death just opened up all old wounds and made them fresh and painful, and I realized after several months, that I wasn't just mourning Alex, I was mourning that time in my life, and my best friend Ellen.

Sometimes, it felt like that time in my life never happened, and other times, it was like it happened yesterday.

I had become delusional and lost all logic. My brains felt like scrambled eggs. I would feel scared because this was not me at all.

No one's death ever affected me in this way. It has been years since I've seen Alex. This was crazy.

At night I would talk to Alex, never knowing if he could hear me, but it made me feel better thinking maybe he could. I would tell him over and over again that I loved him and how much he meant to me. I desperately wanted him to know that.

I would also ask him to come to me in a dream or in spirit, just so I could see that smile one more time, I could live the rest of my life on that. I began reading books on life after death, and reincarnation that gave me hope. These books changed my whole outlook on death and my faith.

If fate was responsible for having our lives cross in this life, I was certainly sure ours would cross again in another life, and maybe this time if given another chance, we could get it right.

Something strange happened to me one morning. I was awakened by someone kissing my lips. I felt it plainly, to the point that I felt the moistness lingering on my mouth.

I was startled by it. Was it Alex answering my prayers? I liked to think so, but I also know that when you are in mourning and grieving someone, these things happen, your mind is on overload, but other things were happening too that made me think that the communications between Alex and I were super strong.

I had so many unanswered questions. They were all answered one way or another that first month after his death.

Before bed one night, I prayed to God and Alex, that if my friend Ellen was still alive, if by some miracle, we could be brought together again. I so needed her in my life now, to help me through the hard time.

Exactly four nights later, I received a call from Kim. She said, "Mom, I think I found Ellen."

All I knew about Ellen was her son's name, and her last name, but if she was married, I didn't know.

Kim gave me the phone number and address and I became excited. I was shaking as I dialed the number. It rang for a long time until someone answered and a voice said, "hello."

☆

I asked "is this Ellen?" and she answered in a cautious manner, "yes, who is this?"

"Is this Ellen that worked at Levanthal's?" She said "yes," excitement building in her voice too, "oh my God. Who is this?"

I answered, "do you remember your old friend Sarah?"

"Walker?" she screamed.

Then I started to cry, "oh I finally found you and I can't believe it!" She began crying too, "you don't know how many times I have thought about you! I thought you were maybe living in another state."

I told her how I had been looking for her for years, and then told her about Alex, I reminded her how crazy I was about him. She said "oh I knew!"

We made plans to meet the following Sunday. I would pick her up from work. She worked in a supermarket only ten minutes from where I lived, and the funny part was I had been in that store on more than one occasion and we never recognized each other I guess.

For the first time in months I was crying happy tears, this was what I needed now and I thanked God and Alex for this blessing.

She told me she would be waiting outside the store for me. She said she now had short hair and wore glasses.

When I pulled up at the store, I saw her standing

with a co-worker. He had a camera ready to capture the reunion.

I couldn't wait to jump from that car, when I did, we ran to each other and hugged, me crying, and her laughing at me, and her co-worker getting it all on film.

We spent the day together, catching up on old times, about all of the friends we had, old boyfriends, and all of the things we used to do together, and on each other's lives.

She had been with her son's father until they broke up and he was found dead in an apartment in New York City.

That's when she began drinking heavily. She said she wanted to be numb. It was the only way she could get through her days.

She had a stay at a rehab and cleaned up. We also got her drug use, while we were still friends, out in the open. She said after she got fired, it got really bad. She began shooting up, and had nowhere to go. Her brother took her in and she started stealing from him to support her habit. Then he kicked her out. That was when she cleaned up her act.

I apologized for not intervening and instead playing ignorant. I explained it was mainly because I didn't want her to feel ashamed.

I was sorry that her life went in such a bad direction, but she seemed okay now. She was working, and had her own apartment. She wasn't on top of the world but she was drug and alcohol free and living a clean life.

We looked at old pictures of ourselves and laughed. We spent the afternoon remembering all the fun times we shared together. I suggested we go to the shore together like old times and visit all the old places we used to go.

I knew that the Moonbeam Ballroom was no longer there; it had burned to the ground, several years ago, which broke my heart. That was a very special place for me. That was where Alex and I first met.

While flipping through a magazine, I saw an article on the "Love Bridge" in Paris.

It is where the people and tourist cleverly decorate the bridge with padlocks to commemorate their love. Pictures of the chain link fence layered with colorful and metallic padlocks spanned the width of the River Seine.

I became obsessed with this idea. I thought, "what a great way to show my love for Alex." A few weeks before Ellen and I took our trip down memory lane, back to Wildwood, I purchased a brass padlock and took it to a jeweler to engrave with Alex's and my name, and the year we met.

I knew that going back to the shore was going to be bittersweet to me, and I hoped I would be able to handle it. I didn't want to be crying all day. I didn't want Ellen thinking her old friend was a total whack job now, but I warned her anyway. There would be a rush of memories coming back I knew, and I had become so fragile, but in a way it would be fun, riding the same bus that we rode so many years ago.

Ellen was the same old Ellen in a way, she laughed constantly just like she use to, but there was a thickness to her now, life had hardened her a bit, but I am sure that I am not the same as I used to be either.

I know I had changed, after the death of Tom, and again after the death of Alex. I went from a strong woman to a pile of soft, sobbing mush and I was not happy with that.

I fought back hard everyday.

I tried to hide my feelings most of the time, especially from Kim, but she could see right through me. She'd say, "it's okay Mom, you take as much time as you need. Everyone grieves in their own way and for some it takes longer."

I had met Ellen at the bus depot, and we boarded the bus for the two-hour ride to the shore. We talked and giggled like two school girls, I confided to her the bad time that I was going through with Alex's death, and I told her that Alex was Kim's father.

She didn't seem surprised, and said, "I thought so. Wow, you sure can keep a secret!" She also said that it was okay for me to feel the way that I did. "You held all of that love for him all of those years, now you're letting it all out."

"I guess you're right." I never felt foolish or silly when I talked to Ellen about Alex. She was the one person who knew how much I loved him.

I told her all about Kim, and we made plans to have lunch someday. "Yes. After all, I would love to meet my Godchild!" she said.

She also told me that she contacted Frank, her ex-boyfriend and they made plans to meet at his apartment where he greeted her with a long-stemmed red rose and a kiss. He made her a great dinner and after, he showed her how to Disco dance.

Now it was my turn to be jealous of her, how romantic, I thought. They had a few dates, but she was smart enough to realize that they were two different people now and it ended. But she said she would love to see him again.

We got off the bus and had a good little walk to the boardwalk. I remembered from all those years ago, lugging a heavy suitcase for blocks in the summer heat.

It felt good just to breathe the salty sea air again. I loved it so much. We reached a small place that had lockers and showers, where we put our belongings and then headed for the beach.

I must have forgotten the walk to the beach from our youth. I don't remember the water being so far from the boardwalk, but Ellen assured me it had always been that way.

I never in my wildest dreams would had ever thought that I would be laying on this beach with my dear friend again, and when not conversing with Ellen, while lying there sunbathing, I was thinking of Alex.

Every now and then a tear would gather in the corner of my eye. After a few hours on the beach, we headed back to shower and change clothes.

I wanted to walk up the boardwalk, to The Dixon Hotel.

When we got there, The Dixon was gone. It had been torn down to make way for the new hotel that was under construction.

So we started walking to the Italian restaurant, where we ate dinner every night, and that was not the same. It had been entirely remodeled and had a different name.

In a way I felt relieved. I think if things were the same, it just would have been far too emotional for me, and would have reduced me to a babbling fool all day.

I wanted this to be a fun day and not a sad one.

We walked back, and looked in stores along the boards. We stopped and Ellen got matching tee shirts for both of us. We took a lot of pictures, and talked some more on the ride bus ride back to Philadelphia.

I told her about my marriage, and the affair that I had with Robbie, about the times that Alex and I met over the years, and about the last dance that we had together.

Ellen commented on how Alex was like my real life Ken doll.

I said, "yes, and believe me all the other girls wanted to play with him too!" and with that, Ellen let out one of her signature laughs.

I told Ellen there was one thing I needed to do when we got to the spot on the boardwalk where the Moonbeam Ballroom once stood.

Sadly, the Moonbeam was destroyed by fire a long time ago. I remember seeing it on the news almost 30 years earlier and I was sad then.

Standing in the Moonbeam's place was a family restaurant now and as I approached the fence on the boardwalk I quietly but ceremoniously said, "I hope this lock stays here forever, my love for you always will." And with that, I clamped the padlock closed.

My hopes were that others would see the lock and do the same, making our own "Love Gate" there in Wildwood.

It was an enjoyable ride home, learning more about my friend, and what was happening in her life for the last forty years.

When we arrived at the bus depot, Kim was waiting for us, and we took Ellen home. I had thanked Kim for staying with my mother for the day, and making it possible for me to go to the shore with Ellen. It had been a dream I never thought I would get to live again.

Ellen and I talked on the phone every week. She would come over and spend a day with me or sometimes we would meet for lunch.

I told her that I wanted to take her to Atlantic City for her birthday in September; after all, I had many birthdays to make up for.

It was another great day; we had dinner and saw a show. We played the slot machines for a little while, and we returned in October for my birthday.

Again Ellen and I planted the friendship seed. Our friendship was a loving, caring friendship that was blossoming once again.

Although I was happy that my friend was back in my life, there was still a piece of the puzzle missing, and would never be there again. It made me feel hollow inside. I still longed for Alex. I still wanted him and I was afraid that I was never going to get over this hurt of him no longer being here.

I would go for weeks feeling good and thinking that I finally had a handle on it, only to have the sadness return with a vengeance.

☆

I suddenly felt the need to memorialize Alex so I decided to get a tattoo. I designed a one of a kind tattoo with the words "Moonbeam Ballroom 1968" in a half circle, and "My Memories Dance," on the other half circle, with a shooting star in the middle with "AB" for Alex Bentley.

I became very excited, as this would give me the closure I needed. I felt that honoring him with this tattoo would work.

I had always been a little shy and awkward about going to a tattoo parlor alone. They were always full of men from motorcycle clubs but I'd made up my mind. I didn't care who was there, I was going.

This wasn't my first tattoo. I had gotten one on my ankle when my husband got his last tattoo. I remembered "the high" from getting it and could easily understand why some people have many. If I were in my twenties, I must say, I think that I would have gotten more, but they're especially nice when they have strong meanings, like this one would have for me.

My appointment was on Sunday afternoon at one o'clock and when I arrived, I was the only one there. That put me at ease. I started discussing the tattoo that I wanted, and showed the artist my design.

While he was critiquing the tattoo, he asked me about it and what it meant. I told him the whole story of losing a friend, and then finding another friend and he thought the story was fascinating.

I had the tattoo put on my left ankle, and it looked great. I went home feeling good. The high lasted about two weeks and the sadness and sorrow were slowly creeping back in.

I would sit depressed, stuck in the past unable to move forward no matter how hard I tried. It was like climbing up ten steps, only to fall down twelve.

During this time, I decided to write on paper my final wishes. If anything was to happen to me, I wanted to be cremated with my picture of Alex and myself. I would want Kim to spread my ashes down the shore at the site where the old Moonbeam Ballroom once stood.

I wanted my friend Ellen to be there too. I had told Ellen this and told her that she was positively not allowed to die before me. To which she replied, "oh ok, I won't."

I want my spirit to be able to remain in that special place forever. Just saying that makes me feel happy and content.

I wrote all of this in a letter to Kim, and told her where it would be when the time came.

I suppose you could say I was blessed, to have that dream come true. To love someone so much was a wonderful gift in itself. To have that wonderful time, that sometime still feels so surreal.

There were many dreams that I had for myself, some never coming true for me, and some did. I think as we age, we all ache for our youth. It's only normal.

I never thought my life was anything but ordinary, until I began writing these memoirs. I feel I lived quite a life, but one thing was true, I was happiest whenever I was dancing!

I would try to dance, even if it was to only one song every day, for Alex, because he no longer could.

He loved to dance and was one of the best dancers in our city.

I know as sure as I am writing this book, that our paths will cross again, in another time or another life. I don't know how, I just know that they will. This may have not been the first time we were together, those feelings when I was just a young girl had to mean something.

Kindred spirits, or something like that.

Months had gone by. It was a sunny, crisp fall day in October, a week after my birthday, and one week before Alex's.

I had stopped at a service station to gas up my car.

After paying I walked back to my car. Something was flying close to my face and circling my head. I began flailing my hands and arms about hysterically trying to shoo away what I thought might be a huge bee, or a dragonfly. But when I reached my car I saw that it was the largest orange and black Monarch butterfly.

I was amazed how beautiful it was. I put the palm of my hand out and kept very still. The butterfly landed in my hand, and opened its wings several times, and then flew away.

I was trembling as I got back into the car. At that moment, I felt the strong spirit of Alex. Maybe he came in spirit as a butterfly because of the poem I wrote about him, and was his way of showing me that he approved of it.

I started to cry uncontrollably. I couldn't even see where I was driving but at the same time I had a feeling of calm and felt peace overtake me.

Sure, it could have been just a coincidence, but there were so many times I would feel his presence. Even in these pages, I had pushed it all back so many times. Putting it off, but I always felt a nagging and invisible push that compelled me to write.

He would have loved a story to be told about him. Alex was no stranger to ego, and I say that with a smile.

I have many people supporting me in my efforts, and I would love to make them all proud of me.

I was the little girl who could not study for her test. The teenager who was told that it would be best to leave school and get a job. I was a woman without self-confidence.

In mid-December, my mother passed away from complications of pneumonia. I was only glad that I lived long enough to fulfill my promise to my dad. I'm sure they are together now.

I am back living by myself. The times I spend alone only give me more time to ponder on my hurt, sorrow and loss. I fight these feelings every day but I feel I am still losing the fight.

I spend time with Ellen and my daughter Kim and I thank God every day for both of them. Sometimes I feel I make them responsible for my happiness, and that is wrong. It's not right to put that much responsibility on someone else, because the only one that can make me truly happy is myself.

I have lost so many people in the last few years, but no one's death affected me as profoundly as Alex's.

He is the first thing I think of every morning, and the last thing I think of every night. I suppose it will always be that way from now on. Although he is no longer here physically, he is always with me, in my mind and, in my heart.

I often think of the times I spent with Alex, and how I took every precaution not to get hurt. How ironic, that I'm now going through the biggest hurt of them all.

I once heard someone say, "hurt is the price we pay for being in love." It doesn't matter. The pain I have to endure now wouldn't be traded for the world.

Having known Alex the way that I did was a dream come true and I feel fortunate to have had my cherished times and memories.

"This was the last entry." As Kim peered up from the tear dropped pages, she looked into Ellen's swollen red eyes, down to her saddened but comforting smile.

Kim looked at her copy of the photograph Ellen took so many years ago. The image of her mother and father kissing at the dance that she chooses to think of as the happiest time in both of her parent's lives.

"I asked Mom a long time ago who my real father was. She was reluctant to tell me, so I never brought it up again. I always knew it wasn't Tom." Kim held up the picture, "I found this once in the closet that used to belong to Mommy at Nana's house. It was ripped in two pieces. As soon as I saw it, I knew who Mom was with and what he was to me."

"She was wild about him, and he was crazy for her." Ellen said, as she hugged Kim tightly.

"It wasn't until Mom found out about Alex dying that she opened up and told me the whole story. She seemed so relieved to share her secret. I have no doubt that her heart just couldn't take missing him anymore and I'm sure her last thought was of him." With that said, Kim gently kissed the photo, placed it in between the pages and closed the book.

They got up from their bench; seagulls were flying overhead as the sun was setting in the bay. The stars were appearing one by one in the indigo sky. The clouds off in the distance were a beautiful sky-blue pink.

"This is exactly how Mom wants this to be," Kim said as she looked at the sky and then to the amusements off to the right.

Ellen and Kim walked hand in hand to the edge of the old pier where the Moonbeam Ballroom once stood. The ashes of the treasured photo was mixed with her mother's ashes as requested. It was time. Kim and Ellen lifted the urn together and tipped it. Sarah's ashes were picked up by the wind, and spun in a small vortex that seemed to dance there for at least a minute before dispersing softly in the air.

Ellen pulled a small envelope out of her pocket, "there's one last thing. Sarah wanted us to read this after we kept our promise." She slowly handed it to Kim and they both started crying hysterically.

Kim opened the envelope and pulled out a little card with a watercolor painting of a Monarch butterfly landing on a rose, inside was a handwritten note:

First, thank you both for keeping your promise to me.
I know Alex and I are together right now so please do not be sad anymore.
In a few months, this beach will be full of people, and it will be summer once again. It may be the year for some new lovers to find each other, and have wonderful thoughts of a love so special that they will remember it for all of their lives. Alex and I will be right here, feeling their excitement and wonder and we will be happy, because this was our special place. This is my special place where I found my one true love, so many years ago.
Summers will come and summers will go. Things

will change, but know that my spirit will always remain against the backdrop of this black summer sky and the glow of the lights from the boardwalk twinkling.

Rest assured this is where I truly want to be.

Love to you both forever,
Sarah

THE END.

Made in the USA
San Bernardino, CA
17 September 2014